Y0-BCN-980

MERCY ROAD

Stories of
South Carolina, Virginia and Georgia

BENJAMIN WIRT FARLEY

Illustrations
Felix Bauer

Cherokee Publishing Company
Atlanta, Georgia
1986

Library of Congress Cataloging-in-Publication Data
Farley, Benjamin W.
Mercy Road.

Contents: The opera house—Utnapishtim Sam—
The heritage—[etc.]
1. Southern States—Fiction. I. Title.
PS3556.A7157M4 1986 813′.54 86-14790
ISBN 0-87797-122-6 (alk. paper)

This book is printed on acid-free paper which conforms to the American National Standard Z39.48-1984 *Permanence of Paper for Printed Library Materials.* Paper that conforms to this standard's requirements for pH, alkaline reserve and freedom from groundwood is anticipated to last several hundred years without significant deterioration under normal library use and storage conditions. ∞

Manufactured in the United States of America
ISBN: 0-87797-122-6

Cherokee Publishing Company is an operating division of the Larlin Corporation, P.O. Box 1523, Marietta, GA 30061

for
Margaret, John, and Bryan

and for
PHILIP H. ROSENBERG
of
ABBEVILLE

The stories in this collection are stories about "real" people and places and events; however, the characters are purely fictitious and the events products of the author's imagination.

At heart, these stories are offered as a commentary and meditation on a way of life that still ennerves a sense of existence unique to the South and to America.

TABLE OF CONTENTS

THE OPERA HOUSE

The Opera House

The debonair gentleman who stood in the recessed entrance of the clacking coach car listened to the train's engine sigh, then hiss, as the engineer brought the train to a noisy halt. A cloud of steam engulfed the engine and rolled back slowly across the coaches.

The man dropped his leather valise onto the platform's pavement and stepped down. He was grateful his touring troupe had arrived.

In less than a fortnight, they had traveled from New York to Philadelphia, from Philadelphia to Richmond, and from Richmond to here. In three more days they would be in Atlanta. But at least the stop in Abbeville would offer a needed reprieve and one final rehearsal before playing before the larger audiences of Atlanta.

This was his first tour with the theatre guild, and he had looked forward to this trip south with a mixture of excitement and remorse.

He had not been south since the closing years of the war and since his brief service of occupation during the Reconstruction. Lumbering over the rails with the guild had brought back memory upon memory, as they had traveled farther and farther south.

He had never been to the Up Country or to Atlanta before. He had seen Columbia and Charleston in the late 1860s and the gutted mansions and gaunt chimneys that Sherman's pillaging parties had left standing in the weeds.

The actor glanced uphill toward the town. It was good to be in a town that had survived that era, that had made it through the entire first decade of the new century.

He picked up his valise and followed his colleagues toward several waiting carriages. He climbed aboard one and scooted his bag under the seat. He glanced up again toward the town.

Abbeville appeared to be built on the brow of a hill. As the carriage bounced along, the actor looked to the right and to the left. The town's old homes, picket fences, magnolia trees, and narrow streets appealed to the romanticist in him.

The street suddenly opened onto the town's square. It was long and broad. A new granite monument, erected in the center of the square, sparkled in the October sunshine. Hardware stores, banks, groceries, apothecary shops, and clothing stores encircled the town's bustling center.

The carriage trundled across the square and pulled up in the entranceway to the Belmont Hotel.

"Yes-suh!" droned a bald-headed, wrinkled old Negro, who was accompanied by a small black child. "Jus' leab yo' bags where they is. Me an' Isaac, here, we'll brang 'em up to yuh 'fo' y'all eben be reg-stu'd," he grinned.

"Was yo' name, suh?" asked the old Negro.

"Hamlin Pursinger," replied the actor. "What's yours?"

"Raf-fi-el, Mis-suh Pu'sing-uh. Now which is yo' bag?"

"The one with the double leather straps," said Pursinger. "It's heavy."

"O, don't fret yo'se'f none o-vuh us," said the Negro. "Me an' Isaac, we use' tuh ha'd wo'k."

"Your son?" asked Pursinger, nodding toward the black child.

"Gran'son!" replied Raphael.

The little boy grinned and began dragging the big valise out from under Pursinger's feet.

The actor smiled and climbed down from the carriage.

Several hacks, other carriages, and a motorcar had met the troupe at the station. A moil of people, luggage, porters, and wagons congested the Belmont's drive.

"This way!" called the guild's director. He was a ruddy-faced, corpulent man, stuffed in a black suit. He was waving a silk handkerchief. "Please, just follow the steps to the lobby. Your room's been preassigned. Dinner's at six. Be in the Opera House by seven. The curtain goes up at eight. Any questions?" he droned.

Pursinger watched his weary colleagues queue up at the door. Many stood in line out on the porch, as the lobby could not contain them all.

He climbed the steps, walked to the end of the porch, and looked back uptown toward the square. He counted two motorcars. Otherwise, wagons and mules cluttered the open spaces. Riders paused at a circular fountain to water their mounts.

He glanced toward the middle of the square and at its still, relatively new, war monument. It was decorated with a small South Carolina flag and a lone Confederate battleflag. He wondered how many dead boys and how many grapeshot mutilated lives it solemnized.

He had joined the Army of the Potomac in May 1864, just three days after the Battle of the Wilderness. He was a boy of nineteen. The only Rebels he had ever seen were the dead ones, or the wounded and the prisoners.

For the most part, the latter two were a pitiful, dirty, and ragged lot. Their eyes were the eyes of exhausted men, of men tired of carnage and the moaning of dying comrades, of men weary of killing and retreating to kill and retreat again. And yet their eyes retained a noble stubbornness, a frightening passion of loyalty to what had been and once was.

Their dirty faces and hollow eyes had terrified him as a young recruit. But those bitter scenes around the battlefields of Richmond had prepared him for the anger, frustration, and suffering he later had to confront in Columbia and Charleston.

He fumbled in his vest pocket for his watch, slipped out the handsome gold-plated piece, and snapped open its lid. It was four-thirty. Time to queue up with the others. Time to register and to rest up before dinner.

In the lobby he received his room assignment and was followed up the stairs by Raphael and Isaac. He tipped the old gentleman a dime and gave the child a shiny nickel.

"Thank you, suh," the little boy beamed.

"Much o-bli'ged," hummed the grandfather. "We hopes yo' stay be pla-sant," he bowed.

"Thank you," replied Pursinger. "I'm confident it will."

He watched the two retrace their steps down the hallway, then he entered his room. He set his bag down by the dresser and closed the door. He hung his coat over the brass end-post of the bed, crawled up onto its high mattress, stretched out, and fell asleep.

He dreamed. In his dream, he could hear the dull pounding of cannon fire far off in the distance. He was with his old regiment. The sounds of battle grew louder. He fell to the ground and hugged his ears with his hands. The pounding of the big guns was deafening.

He could hear the rap-tap-tap of gun fire. Someone was calling his name. "Pu'sing-uh! Pu'sing-uh!"

He woke up. Someone was pounding on his door.

"Wake up, suh!" called Isaac. "You hast missed yo' dinnuh. An' the dee-rector say to come to the Op'ra House uh-mediately!"

"I'm coming!" Pursinger answered. He rose, opened the door, and handed the child a quarter.

"Lan' o' Goshen!" whistled the little boy, as he pocketed the coin. "You bet-tuh hurry, suh," he grinned. "It done be qua'tuh pas' seven."

Pursinger slipped on his coat, rubbed the child's head with affection, and asked, "How fast can you get me there?"

"Less than uh minute!" replied Isaac. "You jus' follow me."

The Opera House was immediately adjacent to the hotel. One had merely to cross Pickens Street to be there.

"Take me to the stage door," said Pursinger.

Which is precisely what Isaac did.

Once he was backstage, becalmed, powdered, and rerobed, Hamlin peeked through an opening of the curtain from one of the offstage wings.

The house was astir with guests. The small, but luxuriant, auditorium glowed with soft lamplight. Noisy patrons visited with each other. Many ladies were donned in the latest fashion.

Hamlin loved the theatre, the titter and rustle of the audience, the hush that suddenly steals across the house at curtain time, and that frantic feeling an actor fights just before uttering his opening lines.

Sometimes it reminded him of stepping up into the battleline, when his company formed ranks, and they ran with pounding hearts and seared lungs toward the flashing clouds of the enemy's lines.

When the play was over, he was pleased to mingle with the guests. The hallway outside the auditorium was jammed with theatergoers. Bearded men in woolen suits smoked cigars and visited with one another. Their wives chatted with other wives, eyeing their neighbors' hats, jewelry, and stylish garb.

Hamlin was about to introduce himself to a group of men when he noticed a very poised and attractive lady standing alone near a flickering brass lamp. He judged her to be about his own age, between sixty and sixty-five. There was an aristocratic gentleness about her, which the lamplight accentuated.

She smiled and eased her way toward a younger, more middle-aged, man.

Deep in his being, Hamlin entertained the momentary premonition that he had met her before, or if not her, the middle-aged man whose forearm she now grasped.

"A great performance!" the younger man congratulated him. "We Abbevillians are delighted and blessed by such plays. Aren't we, Mother," he addressed the woman.

"Most certainly," she replied, studying Hamlin's eyes and gaze closely. "Harrison and I attend at least two or three performances a season."

"That's true," replied her son. "Tell me, Mr. Pursinger, I've heard that our stage is almost identical to the ones in Atlanta and Richmond. That even the sets are alike. Only the size and audiences differ."

"I've been told the same," Hamlin smiled. "But I can't speak of the Atlanta stage, as this is my first tour with the company."

"You have been south before?" inquired the lady.

"Yes, a long time ago, when I was considerably younger," Hamlin answered.

"No doubt, during the war?" commented the son.

"Yes," Hamlin acknowledged. "A long time ago."

"My father, Captain Harrison Hunter Perrington was killed at the Battle of Cold Harbor. I never knew him," said the middle-aged man. "I don't suppose you ever met him?"

"No," answered Hamlin. "I remember the wounded near Mechanicsville and Richmond and later at Petersburg, but I don't think I ever met a Perrington."

Hamlin's eyes met the widow's. Time had eased her loss, but he could detect remnants of sorrow in her jejune, but beautiful, face.

"Forgive me, Mrs. Perrington," he nodded in a slight bow. "Let us speak of the present. You two must come north sometime. Our cities and mountains and farms are every bit as beautiful as yours. At least they are in Pennsylvania," he laughed.

"I was in Richmond, once, just after the War," said Mrs. Perrington. "I went north in search of my husband. He was reported missing after the Battle of Cold Harbor. I had hoped to find him in a hospital. But it was all in vain."

Suddenly, Hamlin felt deeply sick to the heart. He knew now where he had seen Mrs. Perrington. And he knew why her son looked familiar.

He could not tell them what he knew. Not without destroying both of them.

Sweat popped out on his face, and he reached in his pocket for a handkerchief.

"Are you all right, sir?" inquired Harrison.

"Yes," he replied. "It has been an honor to meet you," he mumbled. "Perhaps I shall see you again," he said meekly.

"The honor has been ours," said Mrs. Perrington, eyeing the actor as engagingly as he was trying now to avoid her.

"Good evening," he whispered. He bowed, turned, and hurried down the hallway, and out into the night.

He gulped the cool air and crossed Pickens Street. He entered the hotel and went immediately to his room.

Once Hamlin was in the solitude and privacy of his room, he slipped his gold watch out of his vest and cupped it in the palm of his hand. The amber light from his room's kerosene lamp caused it to glow with luster.

He angled the watch so that the deftly designed palmetto tree etched on the shiny cover was distinctly visible. He snapped the case open and stared at the initials engraved on the inside lid. "H.H.P.," he whispered aloud.

He had taken the watch from a young, dying Confederate officer, who had been assigned to a forward post, the morning of the first day of the Battle of Cold Harbor. A bullet had pierced the Rebel's throat, and he was strangling to death on his own blood. The man's legs had been splintered by rifle fire.

The young Hamlin had plunged his bayonet into the man's ribs, blessing him with death. He had seen the watch, picked it up, and run on, but not before glancing back. As he did, the dead man's head slumped to one side. The vision of that angular face and its bleeding mouth had returned to haunt Hamlin time and again.

And that young woman at the hospital! "Are you sure a Captain Perrington isn't here?"

"No, ma'am," he had assured her. "I've been assigned here for four months, and we haven't ever had a Perrington brought in."

Hamlin stared at the watch. How could he tell her? How could he divulge that it was he? Yet, how could he go on carrying Perrington's watch, having met his widow and his son?

"What shall I do?" he asked in a hushed whisper.

He went to bed that night in a state of anguish. He fell to sleep only toward early morning.

By breakfast, he had determined what to do.

He was about to descend the hotel's porch, when he saw Raphael coming up Pickens Street.

Ah, he thought to himself. I will ask the old Negro if he knows where Mrs. Perrington lives.

"Good morning!" he called to Raphael.

"Fine! I fine," replied the wizened figure.

Hamlin hurried down the steps and approached the old gentleman.

"I need to find a Mrs. Harrison Perrington," he explained. "Have you the faintest idea where she might live?"

"Fain'est idea?" whistled the old Negro. "Mis-suh Pu'sing-uh, I use' to be that wamun's slave. Yes-suh! But that was lange ago," he droned. "Long 'fo' the wah was ov-uh.

"Po' Mas-suh Peh-in-tun! He never come home. M's. Peh-in-tun, she jus' live alone af-tuh that. Jus' her an' the baby. I stayed on fo' a lange time. Then I was given my free-dum. At fust, I didn' wanna go, 'cause that was the on-ly home I knowed. But free-dum be a pow-uh-ful force.

"Yes-suh, I know that lady," he smiled. "She live up on Pink-ney Stree'." He paused and pointed uptown, toward the north end of the square. "I kin takes you there, if you wan's to go."

Hamlin knew he could not call upon Mrs. Perrington unannounced.

"Wait a minute," he said.

He reached in his coat, slipped out his wallet, and handed the old porter a business card.

"Please take this to Mrs. Perrington. Tell her I humbly request the honor of calling at her home. That I have some urgent information about her husband that I think she and her son would value. Tell her that I can come today, whenever it is convenient. And tell me what she says."

"Yes-suh!" hummed Raphael.

Hamlin pressed a quarter in the old colored man's palm.

"Than'ku, suh," bowed the Negro.

"I'll be waiting for you on the porch," Hamlin said.

Hamlin watched as the old porter made his way up the street and out across the square. He turned to go up on the porch, but he was too restless to wait there.

He crossed Pickens Street and wandered uptown. He passed the Opera House, the courthouse, and paused midway up the street to gaze out at the tall Confederate marker. The monument seemed so bleak, though it gleamed in the sun.

He ambled on up the street and paused outside a large department store's window. He gaped in at the goods. He crossed a narrow street and noticed a tiny jewelry shop to his right. He entered and bought a small velvety box which he slid into his right coat pocket.

He wandered back down the square and stared again at the solemn obelisk. He decided to walk out and read its inscriptions.

"Erected by the Daughters of the Confederacy of Abbeville County, 1906," he read to himself. No wonder it was so new!

He walked about the monument and glanced at a second inscription:

On Fame's eternal camping-ground
Their silent tents are spread,
And Glory guards, with solemn round,
The bivouac of the dead.

He knew the poem from which the fragment was taken. It was a poem as dear to northerners as to southerners and as appropriate for the Union fallen as for the Reb. He had heard it quoted at many Union funerals and had often been called upon by widows to recite it at the graveside of veteran comrades.

Segments of it floated to his consciousness, and he whispered them aloud:

> The neighing troop, the flashing blade,
> The bugle's stirring blast,
> The charge, the dreadful cannonade,
> The din and shout, are past, . . .
>
> The muffled drum's sad roll has beat
> The soldier's last tattoo;
> No more on Life's parade shall meet
> That brave and fallen few.

How ironic, he thought, that the living turn the deathrows of battlefields into something noble and pure, in order to atone for the anguish and horror of slaughter!

"Mis-suh Pu'sing-uh! Mis-suh Pu'sing-uh!"

It was Raphael. The old Negro was crossing the square.

"'Cahm at once!' she say. She be r'ady to see you now!" he announced.

"I'm coming," replied Hamlin.

The two hurried up the square to North Main, turned left at Pinckney, and walked down the block toward the brow of the hill. Hamlin followed Raphael until the old Negro paused at the edge of a handsome yard, guarding a small, but stylish, Victorian house.

"You bes' go by yo'se'f," said Raphael. "M's. Peh-in-tun be mighty e'cited. I goin' back to the hotel."

The old Negro nodded his respects and turned away.

Hamlin slipped the watch out of his vest pocket, nervously untied the fob, and pressed the gold case tightly in his hands. Then he fumbled in his right coat pocket for the jeweler's box, opened it, and placed the watch carefully on a folded felt pad. He closed the box and stuffed it in his pocket.

He mounted the steps to the porch and rang the doorbell. A wave of sickness rose up from his stomach and burned the back of his throat.

The door opened. It was the younger Harrison.

"Please come in, Mr. Pursinger," he said. "We have anxiously awaited your coming. My mother is in the parlor. Please, this way."

Hamlin entered the hallway and followed Harrison into the parlor.

Mrs. Perrington was seated on a sofa. She rose to her feet when she saw him. She was dressed in a black skirt and a pleated white blouse. Her face was pale. She was visibly trembling. She clutched a handkerchief in her hands.

"Please, come in," she welcomed him. "Tell us everything you know. Please, sit here," she motioned toward the sofa. "Oh, what is it you know?" she asked apprehensively, as she reseated herself.

Hamlin sat beside her. Harrison sat opposite them in a circular-back chair.

"Mrs. Perrington. Mr. Perrington," he began. "I don't know how to say this, but I, I am the man who last saw your husband, your father, alive.

"It was at the Battle of Cold Harbor. We were running forward when I saw him. He was wounded, dying.

"I was just a frightened boy. A young recruit myself.

"I cried aloud and stabbed him with my bayonet. I killed him," Hamlin whispered. "It was I," he said. "I."

Tears filled Mrs. Perrington's eyes. Harrison looked stunned.

"O dear God!" sighed the widow, as she pressed the handkerchief to her eyes.

"How do you know it was my father?" asked Harrison. "Did you see his wallet? His name?"

Pursinger raised his hand, as if he could not answer and needed time to search his own soul for what to say next.

"I know," he finally said. "Here." He reached into his pocket and handed Mrs. Perrington the box. "Please, take it," he implored her.

Mrs. Perrington looked at him, frightened and with caution.

"Please," he said, putting the box in her hands.

She took it and slid the lid off and stared at its contents. "Oh!" she gasped. "It's your father's watch, Harrison. It's the watch my father gave me to give him when he left on the train."

She held it up for her son to see. Then she rubbed her cheek gently across the tiny palmetto tree, snapped the cover open, and cried when she saw her husband's initials.

Harrison came to his mother's side and both wept quietly together.

"I'm sorry," Hamlin muttered.

"Oh, no," groaned Mrs. Perrington, as she reached out and took

Hamlin's hands in her own. "It was the war. It was the war that took Harrison from us. Not you," she whispered.

Yet it was he, he wanted to reiterate. "Please forgive me!" he begged. . . .

When he returned to the square, he paused again to stare at the tall war monument. Instinctively, he slipped his right thumb into his watch pocket. The emptiness there was as great as the emptiness he felt in his soul.

He remembered another fragment from O'Hara's poem, and his heart seized upon it for what refuge it could offer.

> Sons of the Dark and Bloody Ground,
>   Ye must not slumber there,
> Where stranger steps and tongues resound
>   Along the heedless air.
> Your own proud land's heroic soil
>   Shall be your fitter grave:
> She claims from war his richest spoil—
>   The ashes of her brave.

He turned and walked on down the street toward the hotel. He could see Raphael waiting for him on the porch.

"Free-dum be a pow-uh-ful force," he whispered to himself.

Indeed, so! his soul concurred, as he waved to the Negro.

Note: Poem quoted is "The Bivouac of the Dead" by Theodore O'Hara, (1820–1867).

UTNAPISHTIM SAM

Utnapishtim Sam

For many years there lived on the edge of our town an old Negro gentleman, whom we all admired. He died in the 1970s, but our fondness for and memory of him has long endured.

He lived alone in a tarpaper shack at the end of a winding lane, which we called "Bamboolevard." The name derived from the fact that dense bamboo thickets bordered the lane and obscured his dwelling from the road. Midway down the lane one also had to ford a narrow creek in order to get to his shack.

In his youth, Sam, as he was called, had worked at the town's oil mill. He helped feed the raw cotton into the gin and ran whatever errands Mr. Willis assigned him.

Sam was a stout, good-natured man. And when he returned to his quarters in the evening, he hitched up his mule, plowed his garden, and tended his cocks.

Sam had a hundred cages or more in which he kept cocks, and he sold them to the white people around town "fo' whut-evuh pu-'poses they'ze sees fit," he allowed.

"No-suh!" he would shake his head. "I don' raise 'em fo' no fightin'. The white folk does that. I jus' raise 'em fo' whut-evuh pu'poses the good God above is dee-signed 'em fo'."

For many years, Sam lived in this manner and pursued his dual vocation: working for Mr. Willis at the oil mill and "workin' fo' the Lawd an' his white folk as gua'dian of all these cocks."

In time, however, an exhausted cotton industry failed, and the law tightened its surveillance of cockfighting. Mr. Willis had to let Sam go, and white folks were leery of buying the big Negro's game-cocks as openly as they had done in the past.

Sam bore these disheartening developments, however, with magnanimity. As he explained to folks in town, "Old Sam be lucky, yes-suh! 'Cause 'tween my ga'den an' all them buh'ds, the Lawd be blessin' me."

Sam's contrition and noble acceptance of his lot endeared him to the town. For white and black folk alike suffered together throughout the Depression and throughout the long decade of hard times that succeeded it. In fact, this was the case long up into the late 1940s.

By then, Sam was beginning to get old. Exactly how old, no one knew. But he had survived. And he had done it all on his own. And by his own wits and strength. And by his indomitable personal character.

"Yes-suh!" he would philosophize. "I has been down an' out. An' the han' of plenty is knocked at the do'."

In fact, black and white people alike often came to visit Sam. They came seeking his advice. And they brought him gifts of food and money.

"Be patient befo'e the good God," he would counsel.

"Lock yo'self in the house when the win' blow out of the eas'. Hug the flo'. 'Cause that win' in the eas' mean that the God above be doin' his wo'k. An' he don't need you outside none to he'p him. No-suh! Jus' stay indo'."

"Yes ma'am, the cock meat be cooked bes' when you age it fo' two days. No. Hang it by its spu's. Yes-am. That's right. Two days."

"Patience. Be patient!" he would admonish the young.

"Go see the preach-uh!" he would advise those in love. "An' may the God above bless you."

"Wo'k!" he commanded the idle. "There be no sub-stee-toot fo' wo'k. Ain't no shame in wo'k. Now, get on down the lane. An' don't you come sneakin' back here none 'roun' my buh'ds. No-suh!"

"Po' it out!" he exhorted the drunks and all those addicted to the bottle. "Throw it away. Let the devil git his own self dizzy an' sick! Shoo-ee!" he would hold his forehead, expressing great disapprobation.

"Be brave! Be brave, my sahn. Be brave, dea' sis-tuh," he would comfort the mourner. "The God of A-bruh-ham, hisse'f, will bless you."

Indeed, the town considered laying a culvert over Sam's creek and graveling Bamboolevard to improve access to the old Negro's shack. Some council members even debated the wisdom of resettling Sam elsewhere.

It was now in the 1950s. Sam still kept a mule and tilled his garden. He raised nearly everything he ate.

His cock cages were dilapidated and overgrown with weeds. Still, he raised a few birds and sold them "fo' whut-evuh pu'poses folks sees fit."

His health seemed sound as ever. His wit and mind were keen. Only his great frame sagged. His shoulders were no longer as square as they had been when he worked for Mr. Willis. And his gait had slowed noticeably.

It was about this time that a pharmaceutical salesman passed through our town and overheard Sam philosophizing at the drugstore. The salesman was impressed with the old Negro and curious about his age.

"Sir, I bet you take some potent formula that you're keeping secret from us," ventured the salesman. "Share it with me, and I'll make you a millionaire."

"E-Lawd!" chortled Sam. "I jus' do my wo'k here below an' lets the good God above do his'n. An' I locks myse'f in the house when it sto'ms."

"Sir, how old are you?" asked the salesman.

"I don't trul-ly know," replied Sam. "I jus' can't say."

"Well, you look like a man with the gift of immortality. I'd say you look as fit as old Utnapishtim did."

"Ut-nuh-who?" asked Sam. "I don't b'lieve I evuh met him. No-suh!"

Everyone laughed, including Sam.

"Utnapishtim?" smiled the salesman. "He was a Sumerian who lived years and years ago. He survived a great flood many years before Noah was born. He built an ark even greater than Noah's. And because he survived, the Sumerian gods blessed him with immortality."

Sam listened with profound interest and puzzlement. He had never heard of Utnapishtim before, let alone about any Sumerians or about an ark greater than Noah's.

"That can't be true," stated Sam. "O' it would be in the Bible. An' I ain't nevuh heard no preach-uh read that name from the Bible. No-suh!"

Still, Sam was engaged by the story. And for weeks after the salesman had left town, he would repeat the name to himself wherever he went. "Ut-nuh-pish-tum! Ut-nuh-pish-tum! Yes-suh!"

In fact, he liked the name so much, he didn't object when townspeople began calling him "Utnapishtim Sam." And the older he grew, the more he favored the name. He thought of himself as having survived the great flood of the Depression and of having been blessed with a longer life than usual.

Now one winter a rain pounded our town incessantly for a week, until the streets' gutters ran white with water. Lawns oozed with the runoff and farmers' fields turned to muck.

Suddenly, someone realized that no one had seen Sam for the past five or six days and that if any street in town were flooded, it surely would be Bamboolevard.

Concerned citizens formed a "search" group, clambered aboard a pickup truck, and rode out toward Sam's.

The curbs were running deep with water, and Bamboolevard looked like a stream. All the town's runoff seemed to converge on that lane.

"We're going to have to go back to town and bring a tractor out here," someone observed.

So the group returned to town. In less than half an hour, three tractors appeared, bulging with men and ropes, followed by a score or more of boot-wearing curiosity seekers.

"Is Sam all right?" people asked.

"They should have put that culvert down years ago!" someone asserted.

"That's right!" concurred the crowd.

"Poor Sam!" someone lamented. "Old Utnapishtim won't survive this."

When the crowd arrived at Bamboolevard, as many as could mounted the tractors, forming a small caravan, and proceeded down the rain-swollen lane.

It took the tractors twenty minutes of sliding and churning to arrive at the ford. But the water there was well over chest-deep, and it gurgled loudly as it swept past.

Beyond the ford, where Sam's tarpaper shack had once stood, was a floating raft of debris, caught against scores of rusted cock cages and privet and bamboo thickets.

"Oh!" groaned the crowd. "Poor Sam. We're too late."

"He must be somewhere under all that junk."

"Maybe not!" someone yelled. "There's an old toolshed beyond that thicket over there to our right. It's back this way in the grove," he pointed. "The tractors ought to be able to make it through the bamboo."

So off through the thicket roared the tractors. And, to be certain, there, about thirty yards beyond the bamboo grove, appeared an old, blackened, moss-stained shed. It rested on rock piers, and its floor was barely above the water level.

As the group drew nearer, two men jumped off into the water and waded toward the front of the shed. To their surprise, they couldn't budge the old door.

"Throw us a rope!" called one of the men. "Here," he said to his companion, "let's loop it over the post and through that crack around the doorlatch."

As soon as this was accomplished, the first man motioned for the tractor to take up the slack and back up slowly.

The tractor strained, the rope tightened, and the door burst open with a rotten splash.

To everyone's surprise, a cock flew out of the shed, flapping its wings and slashing the air with its spurs. And there in the shed, seated on his mule, was Sam, with two or three cocks perched in the shed around him.

"Sam!" they shouted with joy. "It's Sam. It's Utnapishtim Sam!"

"Sakes alive! You crazy pee-pul!" Sam shouted with terror.

"Whut ah you po' white folk doin'? Go home an' lock yo'se'f in the house. 'Cause when the Lawd be doin' his wo'k, he don' need nobody outside to he'p him!"

"Sam! Utnapishtim Sam!" his rescuers continued to exult. "O Sam!" they hailed him with jubilation, as they clambered into the shed and hugged the old Negro and his mule.

THE HERITAGE

The Heritage

Only the slate porch remains—along with the four bases that supported the tall, cast-iron columns. Those graceful, neoclassical cylinders had been cast in Charleston, and the portico they embellished had welcomed travellers to our town for years.

In fact, the columns were visible for over two miles away to traffic coming in from Greenwood. They remained in full view as one approached the house, until one had to turn on Main Street before proceeding uptown.

Now the house and columns are gone. A visitor to the slate porch, however, can still trace the home's foundation in the weeds. One can also catch a glimpse of an occasional twisted and rusted pipe protruding from the soil.

Known as "the Heritage," this house was one of our town's proudest landmarks. It was built in 1849 and was occupied continuously by the same family until the late 1950s.

Then one misty, February morning, a fire ravaged it, destroying its furniture, mementos and all. Even the columns were lost. They were discovered, buried in the hot ashes, twisted beyond salvaging.

Our townspeople were stunned by this special tragedy and, to this day, mourn the absence of this grand home and the powerful role it played in forming their self-awareness.

But let us begin at the beginning, and tuck away, for the moment, this *"in medias res"* introduction. For the true focus of this story is not so much this house as it is its last occupant and her family.

That occupant was a spry and irascible soul, whose petite stature was the anomaly of the proud spirit that indwelled her. Her name was Presly Greer. But the townspeople simply called her "Miss Prissy."

And "prissy" she was, at times. For she spoke whatever was on her mind and did about what she pleased. For example:

It was in the spring of 1940, and she was walking uptown on her way to the post office. As she approached the hardware, she noticed two elderly black men basking themselves in the sun on a bench outside the store.

"Well! Well! Well!" she stopped and glared at them. "There's yard work to be done all over this town. And you? Look at you! Perched here like crows on a fence! Waiting for corn to fall in your laps."

"E-Lawz!" they hissed, making a sizzling sound with their teeth.

"Dat's a fac', Miz Pres-ly," replied the stunned elder of the two, "but ain't you bein' jus' abit ha'd on us?"

"Yeah!" his companion intoned. "We done wo'ked all de good Gawd showly in-ten-dud fo' man-kine to do!"

"That's right!" was her riposte. "For *man*kind to do!"

"Yes-am!" they nodded, dumbfounded, but respectful in her presence.

Then, after she had promenaded on down the street, the elder of the two laughed, "O Lawd! If she ain't be woun' up tuh-day!"

"Yeah! Dat ole feisty hen!" his companion chortled. "Look at her go!"

"'*Crows* on a fence!' Ain't she be some-pun?" the first gentleman allowed. "E-Lord!" he chuckled.

"'Miz Prissy!' 'Miz Prissy!'" the two chanted to themselves, savoring the sound of her nickname.

Miss Prissy was far from arrogant, however. Nor was she always prissy. Sometimes she could be very mellow, very affable. And again, very vain. She simply had an awareness of herself that is rare in persons today.

To an outsider, her whole life seemed wrapped up in the past; namely, her family's. If she had an authentic life of her own, one had to conclude that it was only because she had chosen to make her life a continuum of her family's.

This she achieved through the art of oral history, the oft-repeated sagas she shared with the young girls of our town's college, and with their beaus when the latter were properly chaperoned.

When the weather was warm, she would tell these stories on her banistered, camellia-shaded side "piazza," as she called it. But when it was cold, she would hold forth in the warmth of her parlor.

She acknowledged that most of her narratives she owed to a

great-aunt, "who died the week of McKinley's assassination," she would always explain.

"Her name was Anna," she would reminisce proudly. "And she was my bold passageway to a bright and glorious world."

According to this tiny lady, the family's lineage could be traced to a Robert Halverston Long, an entrepreneur of English stock.

"He was a noble ancestor," she would boast, flashing a pleasant smile at her guests. "He came south from New England in 1790, along with his wife and three young daughters, and purchased land in Virginia.

"Actually," she would confide, with some embarrassment, "he acquired an estate confiscated from a loyalist who had fled to Canada.

"It lay along the James River, just south of Williamsburg, and was scarcely a three-hours ride on horseback from the Plains of Yorktown, where Cornwallis, you know," she would relish condescendingly, "surrendered to Washington.

"It was called 'Fairview,' and like most of those old Virginia homes, it faced the river.

"Aunt Anna remembered visiting it as a girl. Carriages, she said, had to enter from the west. They swept proudly past wide iron gates hung from massive piers.

"A grassy lawn sloped off toward the bluffs," she would gesture in a sweeping motion with her hand. "Pines, poplars, oaks, and dogwoods adorned the grounds.

"The walls of the mansion were a rose-colored brick, Aunt Anna said. And the steps to the front door mounted upward in the form of a pyramid. Imagine that!" she would exclaim dramatically.

"The interior, of course, was as handsome as the exterior. From a fabric-paneled hallway, an elegant stairway ascended to the second floor, where luxuriant rooms opened onto a central hall.

"The walls of those upstairs rooms were beautiful, said Aunt Anna. They were richly wallpapered. Plasterworks decorated the ceilings. Large mantelpieces framed the deep fireplaces. Polished brass gleamed from all the doors. And a chandelier swayed in the master bedroom.

"And if that wasn't enough, Aunt Anna used to say that lovely shafts of light streamed into all the front upstairs rooms. And that one of the hall windows, in particular, provided an awesome view of the James. For sometimes the river flowed blue with sunshine and clear skies. And in the evenings, it rippled silver and red with sunsets."

"O Miss Presly! How wonderful! How absolutely wonderful!" some young coed would interrupt excitedly. "Did you ever see the old homeplace yourself?"

"O no!" would come her solemn and definitive reply. "It was shelled by the Union fleet and burned during McClellan's retreat down the peninsula."

The utterance of this disaster often signaled an intermission. And for the next ten minutes or so, Miss Prissy would settle back in her chair and relish the excited chatter of the girls and note the playful glances of their beaus.

Finally, she would resume her story. . . .

"Mr. Long, who was my great-grandfather, was a wise and prosperous planter. At one time he owned over seven hundred slaves!" she would say, arching her thin eyebrows.

"In fact, by 1796, his crops, horses, hogs, and timber were yielding such high profits as to make him the envy of his neighbors.

" 'And that,' as Aunt Anna used to say, 'is when his troubles began.' For the planters resented his hard work and good fortune. They especially envied the fact that he could still draw upon so many successful ties with his old New England friends.

"Then came the summer of 1797. Malaria swept across the peninsula. And by the fall, its inhabitants were succumbing to that dreaded malaise.

"In a single month, he lost thirty-seven of his ablest field slaves. Then he lost his two tiniest daughters. Last of all, he lost his wife, Sarah.

"That tragedy broke his heart, said Aunt Anna. Even more so, it broke his will to remain in Virginia. Which is what occasioned his resolve to relocate."

"O how sad!" someone would observe. "How lovely and how sad!"

"Yes," their proud hostess would intone. "But we Longs and Greers have learned to live with Providence. . . .

"Now, Mr. Long came to Charleston in 1798," she would continue. "He was a wealthy man by every standard and a *true* aristocrat!" she would assert.

"He was certainly not like the nouveaux riches, whose midlands estates were then producing cotton, while their owners were conniving their way into the upper ranks of Low Country society.

"Mr. Long was accepted into that elite class as one whose credentials were illustrious!" she would almost chirp.

"Aunt Anna said that for the next few years, our great ancestor—who was her father—owned and operated a cotton warehouse on the Cooper River. Later, he bought a plantation along the Santee.

"This plantation had been used during the eighteenth century to raise indigo. But since the British were the major buyers of indigo, and no longer purchased American indigo after the Revolution, the indigo market simply crashed.

"Besides, it was now cotton. For cotton was the new king.

"Why, did you know that in those days our state produced half of all the nation's cotton?" she would ask.

"Why, no!" would come a chorus of replies.

"Well, we did!" she would answer emphatically.

"Where did your family live, then, Miss Presly?" someone would ask.

"Why, near the bay. Of course!" she would reply.

"Aunt Anna said that Mr. Long lived in an old Georgian house, just off Tradd Street. It was just a pleasant carriage-ride's distance from his warehouse.

"But let me return to the story. . . .

"My Great-aunt Betsy—Mr. Long's surviving daughter—was then sixteen. She was completing her education under a lovely Huguenot lady, whose family had come to Charleston in the late 1680s.

"This family had never risen to great wealth or position. But this lady's mother had opened a school for the *jeunesses* of the city.

"The lovely lady who was directing the school was a Claire Maros. She was the young widow of a French officer who had served with Lafayette. After the Revolution, this officer had returned to Charleston, but had died the following winter of a fever.

"Aunt Anna said that her father fell in love with Mme Maros the first day he escorted Betsy to school. But he concealed his love from her until Betsy had completed her courses. Then he called on the lady and ultimately proposed to her.

"This charming young widow became Aunt Anna's mother and *my* great-grandmother," Miss Presly would smile, pleased with the excitement this declaration evoked.

"Aunt Anna was born in 1805," she would continue. "A year and a half later, my grandfather, Captain Davis Charles Long, was born. Then two years later a third child was born—a little boy—and with him, tragedy. For he was a breech birth and died. And with him died the lovely Claire Maros."

"O how horrible!" someone would exclaim. "How utterly horrible!"

"Yes," was all Miss Prissy would reply.

"Aunt Anna was barely three-and-a-half at the time," she would resume. "But she could clearly remember the black coffin, her mother's gray face under the veil, and her father's open grief.

"After that, Mr. Long took to alcohol. He entrusted the children to Betsy's care and gave himself up to dissipation.

"He began gaming and carousing with Charleston's beau monde. It was a time of 'high life,' and he indulged himself fully.

"Nightly, he gathered with other gentlemen and played cards and dice. He pursued a deliberate path of folly. It was as if he wanted to block out of his soul all that he had once loved.

"He became self-indulgent. He grew extravagant in his losses. He surrendered his warehouse with a single roll of the dice," she would exclaim gravely.

"The next morning, they dragged his body out of the Cooper. He had shot himself before tumbling off the wharf near his warehouse. His horse was still waiting for him at the hitch."

"O dear!" her guests would groan.

"Oui!" Miss Prissy would concur. "It was very sudden and very sad.

"After that, Betsy sold the house near Tradd Street and moved with Anna and the tiny captain to the plantation on the Santee.

"Sometime around 1810, she met a planter from the Long Canes at a Christmas dance in Columbia. His name was Louis Pedigru. He was a young, back-country gentleman of modest wealth. And how he fascinated her with his riding ability and daring tricks!

"He had a horse that could jump two bales of cotton laid end-to-end. And he was so agile on a horse that he was at home on it, saddled or unsaddled.

"Not long after Betsy had met Mr. Pedigru they were married," she would smile. "And so it came about that our tiny family made its way to the Back Country."

At this point, Miss Prissy would draw a sigh and would often announce, "Let's have refreshments!" Then she would busy herself with cups and napkins, demitasse spoons and tea. Indeed, she was not above serving leftover biscuits and honey, if any were on hand. And if it were in the fall, she might even pour her guests a cup of cider that she had pressed herself.

"Now don't tell anyone!" she would threaten them, feigning a scowl, as she poured the amber liquid into their cups.

After everyone seemed relaxed and had settled back in their chairs, she would continue her *belle histoire.*

"Mr. Pedigru was truly a spirited, back-country planter," she would assert. "He brought Betsy, Aunt Anna, and the Captain to 'the Pines,' as he called his plantation in the Long Canes.

"Aunt Anna was a child, going on seven. But she could remember her half-sister's shock upon viewing Mr. Pedigru's plain, log house for the first time.

"Oh, to be sure, it was a fine house!" Miss Greer would reassure everyone. "For its logs were notched and carefully hand-hewn. But remember that Betsy had grown up at Fairview, and had been exposed to the fairest and most cultured city on the seaboard during the most impressionable years of her life.

"One can imagine the difficulty with which she must have adjusted to that rough plantation existence of the Up Country! But, then, the Longs have always been able to take adversity in stride," she would boast with acerbity.

"The young Mr. Pedigru fancied himself a society person, Aunt Anna used to say. And so he busied himself and his bride with refurbishing the house's interior and hosting rounds of entertainment.

"Then came the War of 1812. And off he went with General Arthur Hayne to fight under Andrew Jackson in Louisiana.

"The brash fool almost got himself killed!" she would state disapprovingly. "Trying to show off with his riding tricks! Two horses were shot out from under him. He lost his left eye when gunpowder exploded in his face.

"But worst of all, he had taken a young cousin with him, a boy who had just graduated from Dr. Waddel's Academy. He had promised Betsy and the boy's mother that he would guard the youth with his life. But the young boy was drowned at a river crossing on their way home.

"It was a saddened and wiser Mr. Pedigru who returned. He was still young and energetic and had that *patch* over his eye! But he cared less about fancy riding and more about becoming a successful planter.

"Aunt Anna said that he became involved in politics and was a major leader among up-country planters who resented the congressional tariffs of the 1800s.

"Now, I realize you children don't know what those tariffs were. But after the War of 1812, Yankee manufacturers wanted their goods protected from the cheaper imports abroad.

"So, in the 1820s, Congress passed tariffs to that end. But the tariffs made it very difficult for an agricultural state like ours to trade with England, or any of the other countries, for that matter.

"Instead, we had to buy all our goods from the North. Cotton prices fell. Yankee goods were high. It was expensive to own slaves. Many plantations simply folded.

"So Mr. Pedigru went about the Long Canes and the Edgefield District, urging repeal of the tariffs. He was very active in the protest of 1832 and favored Mr. Calhoun's nullification program.

"He even went North in 1828 to Washington, to visit Mr. Calhoun, and took Betsy and Aunt Anna with him. It was on their way back that they visited Fairview and Aunt Anna was able to see that gorgeous old home overlooking the bluffs.

"But things soon turned for the worse for Mr. Pedigru. In 1834, while on a visit to Columbia, he was challenged to a duel by some hot-headed Unionist.

"Mr. Pedigru hardly took the man seriously and tried to ignore him. But the other man became incensed. So he struck Mr. Pedigru a violent blow on the head with his whip.

"This caused Mr. Pedigru to have a stroke, from which he never recovered. He died in 1839."

A sadness would now prevail in the room. Miss Presly would lift her small face upward and speak in an almost monotone voice. Here eyes would sparkle. But it was the sparkle of tears.

"Betsy lost her mind after that. She simply grieved herself to death and was laid to rest beside Mr. Pedigru in the family cemetery near Mount Carmel.

"As for my grandfather, Captain Long, well, he died in 1887, at the age of seventy-nine. I was a child of five and have but the vaguest memory of him.

"Aunt Anna used to say that the captain was a scholarly man. He had studied Greek, Latin, and French, and algebra and geometry at Dr. Waddel's Academy and had thought of going on to Yale to complete his education. But Mr. Pedigru, who was more like his father than a brother-in-law, encouraged him to remain in South Carolina and to attend the South Carolina College—which is, of course, the University now.

"My grandfather did and returned to the Up Country, eager to apply his new knowledge of engineering and soil conservation to the tired land and backwoods of Mr. Pedigru's plantation.

"Aunt Anna said he was only moderately successful. But he was a prominent organizer of the Agricultural Society of the Long Canes.

"In 1839, however, after Mr. Pedigru's death, my grandfather became disenchanted with agriculture. Aunt Anna said that he often discussed with her the possibility of selling the Pines and of investing their money elsewhere.

"Then came the War with Mexico. He was thirty-nine. He had never travelled extensively or engaged in activities other than farming and occasionally surveying property in the Up Country.

"After considerable forethought, he volunteered and was among those one thousand proud Palmettos who sailed off for Veracruz.

"He rarely talked about it afterwards, said Aunt Anna, but his heroic regiment distinguished itself in all the major battles," she would assert proudly.

"Colonel Pierce Butler from Edgefield was its commander. This noble gentleman had been a friend of Mr. Pedigru's and had personally picked Mr. Long for service on his staff.

"My grandfather accompanied the colonel closely and was at his side at the Battle of Churubusco when the colonel was shot in the brain and died.

"Fifteen minutes later, Captain Long himself was struck in the knee by a ricocheting cannonball. It spun him around and he collapsed near the mortally wounded Colonel Dickenson.

"Aunt Anna said that he could never forget that long wait beside the dying colonel, as the battle raged on around them. One hundred and thirty-seven brave Palmettos died that day.

"Captain Long lost his leg. But, after the stump had healed, he designed, himself, the wooden peg he wore.

"He was very proud of having fought in the war and was among the few who survived to receive the state's Medal of Honor afterwards.

"Upon his return to the Up Country, Captain Long married a lady from Abbeville—a Miss Lillian Presly. The following year, in 1848, my mother was born.

"My grandmother Lillian didn't like the Pines. She worried that with the loss of the captain's leg, overseeing the plantation would put too great a burden on him.

"Thus, she, Aunt Anna, and my grandfather finally agreed that the Pines ought to be sold and that the family should move elsewhere.

"About that time, the college needed someone to teach mathematics and algebra. Grandmother Lillian knew the college's president and persuaded him to offer the position to the captain.

"Thus the family sold its small plantation in the Long Canes and moved to DeWitt and built this fine old home," she would sigh.

"When the War Between the States broke out, the captain was fifty-three. Enthusiasm for the war was very high. But my grandfather had seen enough death and could never forget that long painful wait in the sun beside the dying colonel.

"Aunt Anna said that, during the opening battles of the war, my grandfather would sometimes don his old regimental coat, medal and all, and wear it to the college. But after Vicksburg and Gettysburg, he put it in a trunk, along with the pistol he had carried in the Mexican War, and never opened it again.

"If anyone ever mentioned it to him, he would reply, *'Sic transit gloria mundi.'* Or, *'Omnia bella sunt luctuosa.'* "

"O what does that mean, Miss Presly?" someone would beg to know.

"'*Omnia bella sunt luctuosa*'? Why, it means, 'All wars are cause for grief,' " she would translate.

"How absolutely profound!" someone would finally say.

Or, "How true!" one of the beaus might venture.

Miss Greer would sigh. "Grandfather died in 1887. Grandmother Lillian died in 1892. My own mother lived to be seventy. But Aunt Anna died the week of President McKinley's assassination . . ."

It would now be late. Sometimes Miss Presly would just sit there, momentarily oblivious to her guests.

It was time for them to leave. Time for them to be chaperoned back to the campus.

Sometimes she might glance up and stare at them, as if they were total strangers, intruders into her private world, which she had not meant to divulge at such length.

But, often as not, she would rise to her feet and invite them into the hallway. She would pause in the shadows of that dark, dank corridor and point up to her family's portraits.

"That's Betsy—the lady there. We don't have one of Mr. Long," she would explain.

"And that! That's Mr. Pedigru.

"Over here is Aunt Anna. And that shy man! That's my grandfather," she would boast. "And there's his trunk!" she would point triumphantly toward the wall. "It has never been moved or opened since his death."

Then she would follow her guests to the door.

"Good night, Miss Presly," the girls would say.

"Good night, to you, too," she would smile. "Come see me again, when you can."

"We will, Miss Greer," someone would reassure her. "Thank you so much, and good night."

"Oh, you're all so welcome," she would snort with pride. "Good night!"

Miss Greer was seventy-eight when she died, or rather disappeared. For she was in the house when it burned.

"It went up so quickly!" neighbors said.

It had been a misty, foggy morning.

"We didn't realize that part of the mist was smoke, until it was too late," they explained.

After the fire was extinguished, no one could find Miss Greer's body. Not even a bone. They raked through the ashes for a week before giving up.

It was a shock and a mystery to everyone.

Then one fall an archaeologist came to the college. He was intrigued by descriptions of the old home and how the house went up in flames so quickly.

He began studying houses of that era. One day he came across a drawing that sent shivers up his spine.

"Was the hallway very drafty?" he asked people.

"O yes!" those who knew replied. "It was always cold and drafty, even in the summertime."

Within the week, he had one of his classes digging around the foundations. He sent a second group to the back of the lot to clean out Miss Prissy's forgotten well. It had been filled in with charred ruins and the old, mangled sections of the once graceful columns.

In the meanwhile he kept tapping the earth with a sounding rod where he estimated the hallway to have been. He would tap, tap, tap, and listen.

Finally, the rod went through the earth in a spot where he knew he had located an underground shaft or a narrow basement. By the end of the week, the class had excavated its way down into a steep chamber, to discover a wide, dank, subterranean passageway that angled off toward the back of the lot.

Its walls were lined with loose, crumbly brick. Rank drafts of mildewed air chilled the stupefied onlookers.

In the hush that followed the excitement of the discovery, one could hear the second group's salvaging operation going on in the well. Their noise echoed eerily up through the dark passageway.

"Quick!" said the professor. "Make me a torch. Or better still, run to the hardware and get us a lantern."

The student who volunteered to go had scarcely returned to find half the town gathered on the porch or scurrying excitedly about the old foundations.

"Please, be careful!" ordered the archaeologist. "The lantern, please! Let him through with the lantern!" he called.

Then the professor, with the student behind him, lit the lantern and entered the passageway. "Wait here," he said to the student.

The student knelt in the dirt and watched the professor crawl into the black tunnel. Spiderwebs glistened in the lantern's glow. The light disappeared and the echo of the professor's grunts were all the student could hear.

Suddenly, the crawling stopped. "O God!" cried the professor. "Quick! Help me! I have found her!" he called. "I have found her skeleton, huddled beside an old box!"

In a quiet ceremony several weeks later, Miss Greer's remains were buried beside her grandfather's grave, near the graves of Aunt Anna and Betsy and Mr. Pedigru.

The trunk was carefully raised and given a place of prominence in a special room in our college's library. There one may come and stare down at the captain's folded regimental coat, complete with his Medal of Honor, and admire the rusted pistol he carried that day at the Battle of Churubusco.

It is fall, and the elm leaves at the back of the lot have turned yellow. I stand on the slate porch and watch as the wind blows them in a light golden shower across the lot's brown crabgrass.

As the leaves sparkle in the sunlight, pieces of Miss Prissy's bright and broken world flit across the screen of my mind and settle like scattered fragments all across my soul.

How I loved hearing her repeat those proud sagas! How we imagined we were part of an America still fresh from the victories of Washington's battles; and heirs of a South that had been bountiful and romantic, profligate and wanton, chastened and made sorrowful by war, and yet had survived into the twentieth century to charm and nurture the deepest recesses of our being!

The twirling leaves finally collapse in a silent column of bright dust that quietly hugs the earth.

I listen to the wind and watch a new shower of leaves ballet daintily to the ground. Then I turn and walk back up Main Street, toward town.

BANNERS IN THE DUST

Banners in the Dust

The old men who gathered for their photograph in front of the tall monument were a rare assemblage of Civil War veterans. They were among a handful of survivors who had served in Orr's Regiment of Rifles of McGowan's Brigade.

Three had donned their ancient uniforms; the other two wore civilian garb. The youngest among them was sixty-five, the oldest was seventy-eight.

They were posing for their photograph following the unveiling of the war memorial, dedicated in honor of the district's men and boys who had fought and died in the War Between the States.

They were not the only group of veterans on hand. The square teemed with many old warriors and remnants of units that had fought with McGowan's Brigade. But the five composed a special group. For they were the sole survivors of the Eleventh Company of Sharpshooters. And they had served together from the time of their arrival in Richmond in May of 1862 to the surrender at Appomattox in April of 1865.

The eldest among them was Franklin DeWitt. He was a well-to-do cotton farmer. He had volunteered at the age of thirty-four. He had been wounded twice during the campaigns and had lost a portion of his left ear. Toward the close of the war he was elected as the company's captain. He was in sound health and was currently the county's representative to the house of legislators.

"Come on, lads!" he said. "Let's look sharp. There won't be many more of these."

He laughed and put his right hand affectionately on the shoulder of the man to his right.

That companion to his right smiled and adjusted the lapel of DeWitt's uniform. Then the man stood at attention himself.

His name was Bradley Hall. He was the tallest among them as well as the youngest. He was sixty-five and had volunteered at the age of twenty-one. He was a lawyer and his father had owned one of the district's largest plantations before the war.

Being the tallest, Hall had been positioned in the center of the group. To his right stood two older veterans, one of whom was also decked out in his uniform.

To the far right of Hall, supporting his lean frame on a hickory cane, stood Zacheriah Donalds. He was seventy-six and in the poorest health of the five men. He had lost a leg at the Battle of Reams's Station in August of 1864, but he had refused to be mustered out of the brigade. After recovering in a hospital in Richmond, he was present with his unit when Lee surrendered at Appomattox.

Between Hall and Donalds stood the fourth aged warrior—Horace Agnew. He was seventy. He was a stout corpulent man, dressed in a handsome vested suit with a beige silk shirt and dark green tie. He owned the largest clothing store on the square, and his family had been in the mercantile business since the mid-1860s. He was bald but sported a well-trimmed gray goatee.

"For our great-grandchildren!" he said, as he glanced past Hall toward DeWitt and the slumped-shouldered figure on the proud farmer's left. "Come on, now, Chester," he said encouragingly to the bowed and somber last companion. "This may be our final roll call."

"I heared ye the first time," replied the grave little man quietly. He tried to stand erect and wiped tobacco juice from his mouth with the left sleeve of his dirty tan overcoat. Then he spat on the ground and repeated the process.

"Now, don't none of you move!" said the young photographer from the town's newspaper. "Just a little to your left, Mr. Donalds," he motioned to the old veteran. "That's it!" he called. "Don't move! It'll be any minute now!" he warned.

The crowd and family members watched proudly as the five came to a sober attention. All smiles disappeared. Many eyes of the onlookers filled with tears.

"Steady!" said the photographer, as he reached up to flash the pan.

The five stood motionless. They were ready. . . .

As Franklin DeWitt waited, Chester's old tan coat and Hall's polished buttons caught the edge of his wavering vision and stirred his soul to memory.

Of all the battles in which they had fought, the Battle of Gaines' Mill had remained the clearest in the proud legislator's mind. It was the first major engagement in which all the units of Gregg's Brigade (as it was first known) had been involved. It was also the first call to valor for Orr's Regiment in particular, and it was the first terrifying test of the Eleventh's mettle under fire.

Franklin could still remember the battle's details with horrifying clarity.

The Federals had hunkered down on a hill, opposite Gaines' Mill, just across a creek. Jackson's army was to the Brigade's left. Two companies of skirmishers from Gregg's First and Twelfth Regiments had been ordered forward. Under sharp fire, they had succeeded in driving a line of Federal infantry away from the mill and from the opposing hilltop.

The remaining regiments, the Thirteenth and Orr's Rifles, had followed the skirmishers down to the creek. Only McGowan's Regiment, the Fourteenth, was not with them. As Franklin remembered it, they were somewhere on picket duty at the Chickahominy.

But there, on the wall of the mill's dam, the four regiments had paused to rest briefly. They had enjoyed some liquors and provisions left behind by the fleeing Yankees, then they crossed the dam and waited for new orders.

The orders came all too quickly, in the form of enemy fire from a pine thicket just above the mill. Franklin could still recall how the entire rifle regiment stormed the thicket and silenced the Federal guns. The frightened survivors then fled across an open field and up the hill, while he and Chester and Bradley, and all the members of the Eleventh, showered them with fire.

General Gregg then ordered the entire brigade to advance up the hill, only to discover that the enemy had withdrawn to a second eminence. Between the two armies lay a deep, marshy ravine. Franklin could still see that Federal officer riding back and forth on the opposing hill, his presence signaling the precise location of his own company of infantry.

A terrific shout went up from the Eleventh when they saw him.

Many sharpshooters tried to bring him down, but he was beyond their musket range.

Suddenly their commanding officer, Colonel Marshall, ordered them to take cover in the grass. His order came none too soon, for an enemy battery immediately opened upon them. A cannonball hissed past and whistled over the crest of the hill behind them.

One of their own battery replied with considerable success, for when they rose to resume their advance, they encountered only scattered rifle fire. They hurried down the hill and crossed the wet ravine.

There they were ordered to rest, for it was then mid-afternoon and very hot. A young growth of pines concealed them from the enemy and offered some shade. Nevertheless, they crouched behind their packs, for the infantry in the woods, at the top of the eminence, kept up an annoying fire against them.

They lay there for about an hour and listened in the distance to Longstreet's guns pounding the Federals. The booming of the Confederate guns seemed far, far back, almost behind them.

Years later, it made Franklin realize how truly vast that battle had been and how tiny was the part his own brigade had played. Yet that tiny part had comprised his world at the time and had consumed him with excitement and terror.

Word soon came that Jackson's men were amove on the left, poised to attack their enemy's flank. Their brigade must rise and storm the eminence.

It was four o'clock. The First and Twelfth Regiments were ordered to advance. Franklin could still remember how the men slipped through the pines and pushed their way through the bramble up the hill. But the enemy's fire proved too severe and drove them back.

At that point, General Gregg ordered Colonel Marshall to take the Rifles and charge a battery, with its contingent of infantry, that had been firing upon them from the right. "Eliminate that source of fire!" the general commanded.

Colonel Marshall rode among them and formed them into three lines. He held two companies in reserve. Two were assigned to lay down alternating volleys of fire. The Eleventh and five others were sent into the battleline. The command to begin the advance was shouted, and the regiment pushed forward.

Once through the brambles, they marched at the double-quick up the slope, across an open field.

The opposing fire was murderous. But they pressed on and crested the hill. They raised a piercing shout and flashed their bayonets in the sun. They captured the battery and began firing at the Federal soldiers. The opposing line broke and scurried for safety through the woods.

Suddenly, a large force of New York Zouaves appeared on their left and fired a murderous volley at them. One-tenth of the entire Eleventh Company was killed or wounded in that single volley.

Colonel Marshall shouted encouragements to keep up their resolve. He ordered them to remain cool and to return the fire. But the Zouaves had taken them by surprise and had halted their advance. The Colonel saw that they had lost the edge and ordered a slow withdrawal down the slope.

Meantime, the First and Twelfth Regiments had been hard pressed. The thickets and briars had slowed their advance to a crawl. With the arrival of the Zouaves, the entire enemy line had been able to regroup. Now they raked the First, Twelfth, and Rifles with deadly aim.

Slowly, the brigade worked its way back down the hill.

Suddenly, a wild cheer burst forth from behind them. It was Colonel McGowan and the Fourteenth Regiment! They had just arrived from the Chickahominy. They hurried across the ravine and rushed forward at the double-quick. They caught the Federal infantry in the open field and poured volleys of fire into them.

The entire brigade now took courage and joined anew in the assault. Once through the brambles, they charged up the slope, firing into the wildly fleeing Federals.

The dead, wounded, and dying lay everywhere. Exhausted by the ordeal, Franklin recalled his own collapse. As he lay there on the brow of the hill, he listened to the incessant rumble of musketry all about, the rattling of small arms in furious volleys, the distant thundering roll of cannonade, and watched the towering columns of smoke and dust that rose in the distance.

He would never, could never, forget the terror of that struggle. The brigade had suffered 140 dead, 714 wounded, of which the Rifles Regiment accounted for 81 dead and 234 wounded. No other regiment suffered as many casualties as theirs. Yet, on that hot, June afternoon, they had claimed their first proud laurels of victory and had proven their loyalty and devotion to their state, their homeland, and to the South. . . .

At the same time DeWitt was lost in his reverie, Bradley Hall's own soul winced inwardly and deeply. For he had many brave and gallant friends who had fallen along the way. Some had fallen in battle. Others had died of wounds afterward. But they were all with him now. In memory.

Most of them had been killed during that first year of the horrendous battles. They were among the first to fall. Among the ablest leaders of the brigade. Among the most distinguished from their districts. Among his family's closest friends and associates.

All of them had been older men. They were like uncles, mentors, brothers, even titans. They had often come to Abbeville, or lived in Abbeville itself. And they had both entertained and been entertained by his family. There was no way the lawyer could forget them, and he had often thought of each of them.

The first to die had been Augustus M. Smith, a lieutenant colonel. He had received a mortal wound at the Battle of Gaines' Mill and had died the following Sunday. He was the First Regiment's second officer in command.

Bradley could still remember his friend's wound. He had been shot in the face and neck in that furious fusillade when the First and Twelfth Regiments were caught in the brambles just below the brow of the eminence where the New York Zouaves had fired point-blank into the Rifles.

Of all the losses that day, his had clearly been the severest. A native of Abbeville and close confidant of Bradley's father, Smith was both a refined gentleman and a tough disciplinarian.

Long after his death, the brigade had lamented his loss. And he, the young Bradley, had spent hours trying to explain it in long letters to the colonel's niece, whom, after the war, he married.

Two months later, fate claimed a second dear friend—J. Foster Marshall, also of Abbeville. He had been a prominent lawyer before the war and had been the district's representative to the state senate. He had served during the Mexican War as a captain in the state's proud Palmetto Regiment and had succeeded Colonel Orr as the Rifles' commanding officer.

He died in battle, within an hour of being wounded, during the enemy's slaughtering assault against the Rifles' position at the Second Battle of Manassas. It was an engagement that had terrified the young Bradley and had taught him how utterly devoid of humanity a battlefield can become.

After repulsing line after line of Federals, the exhausted Rifles had resorted to hand-to-hand fighting, clubbing, beating, stabbing, and trampling their opponents into the dust. With wild cries and tears, they hacked and flailed at their assailants with stock and blade until night enveloped them and the enemy was ordered to withdraw.

Other noble friends also crowded onto the stage of his thoughts. Colonel Dixon Barnes, wounded in the thigh at the Battle of Sharpsburg, dying three days later. General Maxey Gregg, commanding officer of the brigade, shot in the spine at the Battle of Fredericksburg, dying the next day.

Frozen in the smoky mist of his memory, Bradley could still behold that incredible general. Time and again, he had ridden fearlessly into their midst, his deep voice rising above the hiss and din of the peril. In full uniform, with his blade pointing toward the enemy, he had rallied them, conquering their anxiety, dispelling their fears.

How it hurt Bradley to recall the brave man's death. For he had been shot during the confusion in the woods near Manassas, where the Rifles had stacked their guns and were waiting for Archer's Tennessee and Alabama troops to pass through. Only the troops falling back weren't Archer's. Instead, they were the first lines of the approaching Federal infantry!

They fell upon the Eleventh and Orr's Rifles before anyone realized what was happening. General Gregg, still believing them to be Archer's men, had ridden hastily between the two lines. He swung his steed about and ordered the Eleventh to restack its arms. At that frightful instance, the Federals suddenly fired. The general's mount reared wildly, and the old man fell at Bradley's feet. . . .

That he himself was here today, alive, seemed unreal. Bradley had the strangest urge to raise his hands and cry into the bloody stains that he knew must still be there.

"Please, hold still!" ordered the photographer, as he took the picture.

"Hooray for Dixie!" someone shouted, amidst a smattering of applause.

"Hooray! Hooray!" roared others.

Bradley shook his head sadly. "They don't understand," he muttered.

The hefty Agnew patted the lawyer on his forearm. The big man's own countenance was grayer and his earlier buoyancy had waned. But he summoned forth a smile and said, "Don't fault them for their devotion. I would do it all over again," he whispered. "And so would you."

"Yes," replied the somber Bradley.

"We all would," added old Zacheriah, as he shuffled about and pivoted on his cane.

"Wait! Please wait!" cried the photographer. "I need one more. Please! Just one more!"

The five turned and looked at each other.

"I reckon we might as well," drawled Chester, as he spat a stream of stringy juice on the ground and wiped his chin with his sleeve.

"I'll need a chair," said Zacheriah. "This is worse than drill," he grinned feebly.

Horace, Bradley, and Franklin smiled and shifted their weight on their feet while someone brought the old veteran a folding chair.

Zacheriah's nephew opened it, and the old man sat down, his cane clutched tightly between his legs.

Zacheriah twitched the stump of his amputated limb and eased his false leg forward.

He had received the wound in the lower part of his thigh. At the time, he thought he would die long before he was carried from the field.

As he thought back on it, the entire little skirmish of Reams's Station had been scarcely more than a probing movement against the enemy's artillery.

They were near Petersburg, on the Weldon railroad. Their area of the front was the extreme right of the Confederate line. Their regiment was still recovering from the exhausting battles of the Wilderness and Spottsylvania Court House.

They had bivouacked about two miles from Reams's Station the evening of August 24, 1864. The battle's full details had never been clear to the old veteran, but as he remembered it, the Eleventh, along with the other companies of the brigade, were wakened early the next morning and marched to within sight of the station.

They could see the enemy in great number drawn up about the junction along the railroad. The Federals had amassed here a forceful array of artillery pieces.

The Sharpshooters were ordered to a nearby hillock, where, from behind its protected woods, they were to disable the enemy's horses and gunners.

Zacheriah had never relished killing animals. And he hated what he did that day.

The company's aim was most effective. They felled every animal near the guns.

Then the Thirteenth and Orr's Regiment were ordered to advance. They swept across the sandy space and fell upon the infantry.

The Sharpshooters were commanded forward. Suddenly, a walloping blow sent him careening sideways. He clutched his leg and fell in the weeds. He rolled over and cried aloud with pain. He could still see his bright blood spurting out on the dry grass.

It was Horace who picked him up and carried him back to safety.

Instinctively, Zacheriah reached up with his left hand and clasped Horace's big right hand. He gripped it tremblingly, then clutched his cane again with his long withered fingers.

Horace knew only too well what his older companion's gesture signaled. The big man put his hand gently on the frail figure's shoulder.

As the photographer motioned for the five to regroup, a horse neighed somewhere on the square. Horace could hear its rider soothe its fears. A carriage or wagon wheel creaked in the distance.

The sound reminded Horace of the tiresome marches and long supply trains that had been an inevitable and inseparable part of the campaigns.

Caught between the sweltering bright days of summer and repeated exposure in the open to prolonged periods of rain, he had become, by the summer of 1863, but a sunburnt, grizzly caricature of his former self.

Of all the campaigns, that year's trail of slaughter and hardship had seared itself most memorably on Horace's soul.

It had begun with the bloody but joyous victory of Chancellorsville and Hooker's retreat across the Rappahannock. Horace could still see the Yankee balloons, hanging lazily above the treetops, the morning before the battle began.

That evening, their regiment's band played "Dixie" and "The Bonnie Blue Flag," while the men sang, well past midnight, to counter the Federal drums on the far side of the river.

After the battle and their grief over the death of Colonel Perrin, they were marched back, west of the Rappahannock, to bivouac and rest before the campaign was renewed.

Then, one warm evening in early June, the order to fall in came. They formed regimental ranks, and, under the quiet of the stars, the brigade began the long march that would carry it to Gettysburg.

In less than twenty days, they marched west to the Blue Ridge, crossed at Chester Gap, descended to Front Royal, waded the cold waters of the Shenandoah, and, on the twenty-fifth of June, forded the Potomac.

What a spectacle that was! Men shouted and cheered as they plunged into the river. Many stripped off their clothing. They sang "Maryland, My Maryland" and marched ashore on the opposite bank in closed-rank columns.

Two days later they crossed the Pennsylvania line. At last, they had invaded Federal soil! (For, as Horace recalled, at the time they all considered Maryland part of Dixie.)

The countryside before them was beautiful. Amber fields of wheat extended everywhere. Livestock, poultry, and gardens seemed in endless abundance. Cherries were ripe for the picking. And whiskey was issued to the army.

Never had their confidence waxed brighter! Their valor bolder!

On the thirtieth of June, they camped at a pass in a range of gentle mountains. Gettysburg lay less than eight miles away to the east.

How it destroyed Horace to think of it now! They were the finest army ever to be marshalled on a field of battle. Yet, in those three harrowing first days of that hot unalterable July, they lost the most critical battle in which the Confederacy ever engaged.

As fate would have it, the Rifles' lot was to guard the pass. The Eleventh was ordered to stay with them. The remaining regiments of the brigade took up their rifles, turned in the pike, and hailed farewell.

For three days they watched from the mountains and listened to the distant bombardment of the heavy guns. They watched the great columns of sulfurous smoke that rose and settled over the gray plain. Late into the night, they could see deadly tongues of fire, flickering back and forth, in furious flashes.

Then, on the morning of the fourth day, the wagons began to trundle by. They passed all day and all night, bearing the wounded and dying. . . .

"Hold your position now!" called the photographer. "That's perfect!"

At that same instant, Chester Lattimar fought off his own reveries. The little scrubby man wanted to spit. But he knew he had to wait until the picture was taken.

The truth of it was, he had enjoyed the war. Downright gloated in it. For years afterward, he had even bragged about the Yankees he had rubbed out.

"Shor, I killed my part of 'em!" he would boast. "Standin', kneelin', or lyin' down, I'd pick out my mark an' shoot 'em like you would a frightened hog. Bang! I'd split 'em right down the middle."

In fact, he could still remember the nervous excitement he relished at the sight of forty Federal corpses, which he counted once, in a single group, wiped out by canister shot.

He had felt the same elation after the struggle of Sharpsburg, when he and some others surveyed the still smoke-enwreathed battlefield and counted the Federal fallen amidst the obliterated shocks of corn, and stared, mouths agape, at the strewn bodies behind the low stone walls.

Sometimes he could still see that mass of glossy blue bodies, clogging the Potomac at Shepherdstown, where the Union dead floated in the water and jammed up around the rocks.

Once, he had even kicked a Federal skeleton (the unburied remains of a soldier from an early campaign), which the company had found in a field along the Rapidan.

But nothing he experienced equalled the insane mood that possessed him after the Battle of the Wilderness. Their own brigade had borne heavy casualties, hence he couldn't help himself when he erupted in shrill cursing at the sight of charred Federal corpses, or hooted with laughter at the stench of the Union bodies whose gases rose through the shallow graves.

The macabre experience only doubled his raw instinct to kill even more lustily in the bloody pits at Spottsylvania.

That attitude had been true of him well up into the 1880s. But now he felt differently.

He couldn't remember exactly when or why the change occurred. But after the hard liquor-drinking days following the war and the bitter years of Reconstruction, he began to feel loathsome and dirty and shameful.

If it hadn't been for Mr. DeWitt (Captain DeWitt after the siege of Petersburg), he guessed he'd have died and gone to hell. But the captain wouldn't accept that. Instead, he kept bailing him out of debt and jail and gave and regave him job after job, both on the farm and at his office in town.

Suddenly, tears welled up in the scrappy man's squinting eyes and trickled down his dirty beard. He was sorry for all the hellish things he'd ever done. But he'd never own up to remorse for what he'd done for Dixie! Never!

Just as the picture was taken, Chester clutched DeWitt's sleeve, almost losing his balance.

The two pictures may still be found in the newspaper's files. The first is posed, strained, Napoleonic.

The second is notably different.

Horace's right hand rests on Zacheriah's shoulder. The old lame veteran sits crouched behind his cane. The tall Bradley stares past the camera, lost in memories of battle. The proud DeWitt stands gallantly at attention, gazing bravely ahead, his faded uniform threadbare at the shoulders. And to his left leans the gritty Chester Lattimar, tugging at the sleeve of his companion's coat.

Of course, the marble monument has also endured. No passerby around the square can fail to notice it. But few bother to read its laurels of devotion to the Confederacy.

On hot summer days, old men sit on the benches beneath the oak boughs that shade the marker. Children play in the grass while their mothers rest or chat. Automobile tires hum and flap gently over the old pavement brick.

Few glance up at the monument. Nevertheless, it looms, Ebenezer-like, in witness to the proud brigades sent north to Virginia, in defense of the Cause. The tall gray obelisk quietly testifies to their ghosts, their valor, and their banners, now long-forgotten and trampled in the dust.

Note: The factual details of the battles in this story are based on J.F. Caldwell's, *The History of a Brigade of South Carolinians* (Philadelphia: King & Baird Printers, 1866). All else is fiction.

MERCY ROAD

Mercy Road

It was good to be home again. Built in the 1820s by his ancestor Captain Mercy Hughes, the plain, square white columns of Mercy Hill still evoked his awe and wonder.

A quaint balcony, protecting French windows above the main door, graced the entrance. A wrought-iron lantern, suspended from an old iron chain, brought symmetry and balance to the long porch.

The steps that led up to the house ascended a steep slope, green with fescue and shaded by cedars, pecans, and elms. Banks of groomed boxwoods bordered its walkway.

Walter C. Hughes could not have been more pleased. Mercy Hill had been his family's birthright since the time of its construction.

Except for a period of thirty years, it had always remained in the family's hands. Its temporary loss was due to the fact that, in the late 1940s, his mother, for financial reasons, had been forced to sell it. A physician from Columbia had bought it.

Fortunately, the doctor's wife disliked the house. She refused to occupy it and had left it untouched. It had taken Walter twenty years to buy it back from the old woman, who had died recently at the age of ninety.

Only one thing tugged at his soul, and that was the loneliness. He hadn't anticipated how lonely the old home would make him feel. For the years he had lived in it as a boy were years filled with family—with his mother and grandmother, with his two older sisters, and with their gossip and chatter, and all the marvel of childhood.

Now, only he remained. And a bachelor at that. Retired and alone. Though he had never intended to become or remain a bachelor.

It was just that college, the war, his career, and other matters intervened. Circumstances, he had always rationalized, had forced him to postpone any marital intentions.

He checked his mailbox. It was empty. He returned up the steps to the walkway and sat in a rocker on the porch.

It was early June. The late morning sky was pale blue. He could see it through the limbs of the elm and pecan trees.

Across the road sprawled a large woods. It occupied a wide, spring-fed gully. From where he sat, he could see out over the woods. In the sunlight, varieties of oak, poplar, and gum trees blended into an undulating web of leaves and silvery limbs.

As a child, he had often played in these woods. They had both beckoned and frightened him. Now he looked out across their green canopy and still felt their summons.

Beyond the woods stretched a patchwork of semicultivated farmland, dense stands of pine, and acres of ill-kept pasture, fallow fields, and broom sedge.

There was a sadness about the land. Walter could feel it in his soul. For this reason, he preferred to remember it as it had appeared in the forties—white with cotton and red with soil and fresh with the smell of rain and hot from the heat of the sun.

A tar-papered tenant's shack had stood just beyond the gully. Nothing remained of it now. It had been the home of a fourteen-year old girl he had loved.

"Ellen was her name," he whispered.

"W.C., Honey," his grandmother would lecture him, "she ain't nothin' but poor white trash. And just a child at that. You're goin' on seventeen and will soon go off to school. There are finer girls in store for you. Just bide your time. You'll see."

Sometimes he would meet Ellen in the woods. Sometimes he met her behind the woodshed near her house.

He never thought of her as "white trash." He knew she was poor. Her dresses always hung too long. But her hair was thick and short, a wild honey color. And her hands were warm, her eyes bright, and her young mouth had always welcomed his clumsy lips.

He wondered if he had stayed, or had come back home after the war, or had not gone north, whether a marriage to her might have worked. There was no way to know. But he doubted if it would have.

A car passed on the road below. Its trunk was heaped with plastic garbage bags, each crammed full. The trunk's raised lid bounced with each jolt the car took.

He knew the car was bound for a pair of dumpsters about a mile down the road.

The sight reminded him that he had resolved earlier to clean out the attic. The old loft was packed with antiques and mementos. But it was also piled with clutter, clothing that would never be worn again, and boxes of junk. Half of it needed to be carted off.

Walter rose, opened the screen door, and entered the hallway. He climbed the stairs and, in one of the back bedrooms, ascended a narrow enclosed staircase to the attic.

With his right hand, he raised a hinged door and hooked it in place against a rafter. With his left hand, he supported himself and crawled out into the attic, then stood.

He turned on the light and glanced down the long, pyramid-shaped loft. The roof's two-by-eight beams had aged and turned a deep orange. The air was hot and redolent of must. The odor of dust burned his nostrils and lungs. He coughed and began to explore about.

There were several stacks of ornate picture frames. Most were chipped or broken. None contained pictures or portraits. One leaned against an old trunk.

Next to the trunk lay a pile of dry-rotted muslin curtains. They lay beside a soiled mattress that mice had riddled. Its cotton stuffing poked through the holes.

Beyond the mattress, swabbed in cobwebs, sat a bottomless captain's chair. Its rungs were split. One was missing.

Farther along lay a dismantled Singer sewing machine. He bent down and ran his fingers across its lint-encrusted plate.

He could still see his mother arched over the whirring machine as she patched his overalls, or stitched pieces of a new dress together for one of his sisters, or repaired a seam in one of her own slips or gowns.

His father had died when he was three. He had no memory of him. It was his mother who had raised him. And his grandmother, his father's mother, who had babied him.

"W.C., honey," his grandmother would chortle. "How proud your daddy would have been of you! My, but you're a big boy!

You're goin' to be so tall! Just like your father." Then she would hug him and kiss him on the neck.

"Go on, now. Get out of here," she would scold him, her eyes moist with tears. "Run along an' play outside."

He wandered on down the attic, squatting occasionally to examine some old comb, vase, calendar, or box of shoes.

Suddenly, his attention was drawn to a purplish-white and brown faded photograph. It was lying in a broken drawer, cocked awry and propped up against the foot of the dresser.

He bent down, leaned forward, and picked up the photograph. It was a picture of himself and Ellen. It had been taken the night of the high school graduation ball.

His mother had made Ellen's dress. It was white and lacy. He stood beside her, tall, somber, dressed in an old suit of his father's.

It was the last time he ever dated Ellen.

"Honey, there's a bevy of high-minded beautiful girls out there. You'll see. Granny wouldn't lie to you. You'll meet them in time."

And, of course, his grandmother had been right. For he met them soon enough at the university, and again in the army, and later in Columbia, and in Atlanta, and in New York.

But the more he became involved in the publishing business, and in the marketing and sales divisions, both of which he came to direct, the less time he seemed to have for himself and for matters of the heart.

He supposed it was just as well. With some reluctance, he returned the picture to its resting place. Then he picked up the drawer and eased it back into the dresser.

He would save this piece, he resolved, if for no other reason than to steal away to it in order that he might stare occasionally again at his youth, and at Ellen's, and at what might have been.

Walter glanced about the musty garret. The air was stifling. Dust coated everything.

He looked at his watch. It was time to eat lunch. Besides, he wasn't properly dressed to be cleaning out such a filth hole.

He would break for a sandwich and glass of tea and change clothes. "Then we'll come back," he said in a low voice to himself.

It was close to five o'clock when Walter made his first trip to the dumpsters. The sun was still high, and it glared brightly against the hood of his pickup truck.

He had backed the truck against one of the containers and was standing in the truck's bed, wrestling with the old mattress, when he thought he heard children's voices. He turned in what he thought was the direction of the voices, but saw no children. Instead, his glance was met by a sloping clay embankment crested with broom sedge and the tops of pines in the distance.

He sighed and heaved the mattress into the sour-smelling dumpster. It hit a broken windowpane, sending up a loud tinkling crash. It slumped and crumpled over.

He thought he heard a child's laugh, followed by another's giggle, then a hushed "shh!" But there was no movement above the bank nor rustling in the dry grass.

It was early evening when Walter made his second trip to the dumpsters. The long June day's sun was sinking into a heavy dusk. Soft shafts of light glinted skyward and bathed a high passing cloud rose-gray.

This time Walter saw the children.

One was a little girl. She was climbing out of the dumpster into which he had dropped the bedding. She couldn't have been more than five or six. She was clutching a soiled pillow he had thrown away.

A tiny boy, no older than two or three, waited for her in the broom sedge at the top of the embankment. He was clad in a dirty undershirt and dirty underpants. He, too, clasped in his small hands some treasure from the pit.

The little girl scrambled up the bank and joined her tiny partner. The two disappeared quickly in the hovering darkness near the pines.

This time Walter unloaded the truck's contents with greater care. He didn't want to damage anything that might be useful to the children.

It was dark when he completed his chore. He drove back toward Mercy Hill, saddened by what he had witnessed.

Walter parked his truck under the pecan trees behind the old homeplace. He climbed the stone steps to the back screened-in porch and walked uneasily toward the kitchen.

He had lost his appetite. He could still see the little girl, dropping like a rat out of the dumpster. The little boy had reminded him of a frightened groundhog peering out over the grass before hurrying away to its den.

He walked to the hallway and out onto the front porch. The evening air was warm. Crickets were singing in the yard, and the frogs in the woods in the bottom had begun their vesper chorale.

He stepped out into the yard and walked to the edge of the slope. He listened to the katydids and frogs until his mind was caught upward by the stars. He descended the steps and wandered out onto the road that he might behold the stars better.

"What is our affinity with you?" he whispered, as he stared up at the twinkling, silent, infinity of the night. "Why are we drawn to philosophize at your sight?"

His eyes roved the heavens until his neck ached.

"How strange!" he exclaimed. Then he thought of the little girl. "What will she do with that pillow?" he wondered.

He took a deep breath. It was better not to think about it. Besides, where would one begin? And if one did, where would such a beginning end?

"Moral defeat," he supposed.

He had once heard a poet at the publishing house lecture on "moral defeat." The poet was in his thirties. Everything the young man had written was being published. What did he know of "moral defeat"?

Walter shook his head. He wandered back up the steps and into the house. He made himself a cup of coffee, brought it out onto the porch, eased into a rocker, and sipped the hot beverage.

He was beginning to feel hungry, and he wanted to eat. But the words of the young philosopher, the successful poet, annoyed him.

"Moral defeat!" he repeated. There was an edge of sarcasm in his voice.

That night he retired to bed with a strange sense of purpose beckoning him. He could not fully explain it. But he intended to return in the morning to the dumpsters and let happen whatever might happen.

The call was as clear to him as if he had received it from the stars. As if the night itself had understood and had been the prime mover behind his wandering out onto the road and his having looked upward.

Very well. He would go.

He rolled to his side, closed his eyes, and drifted into sleep.

The next morning, he rose early, dressed, and hurried down to the kitchen. He ate a light breakfast and carried his coffee out onto the porch.

The morning sky was clear. The sun's waking rays filtered through the trees in bright shafts of light. A chipmunk scampered across the walkway and buried itself noisily at the base of one of the boxwoods.

Walter sipped on his coffee and paced the long porch. If the children were desperate enough to salvage dry-rotted bedding, then what other needs might they have?

Perhaps he should put a few food items in a small box and place it where the children would discover it.

He walked to the east end of the porch and stood in the sun's warm beams. It was too early to go yet, but perhaps he should scan his cupboard to see what staples he had.

He didn't want the box to appear to be too "planted," so he searched his shelves for half-filled boxes and containers of cereal, cookies, flour, shortening, grits, beans, cornmeal, jelly, bread. He soon had two small cardboard boxes packed tight with goods.

That should be enough, he thought.

He dropped in a few sticks of gum and some hard lemon drops, which he kept in a small candy jar for his own occasional indulgence.

Hopefully, that would whet their appetites.

He was halfway across the back screened-in porch when he realized that rats and flies would swarm all over the boxes unless he could attract the children's attention almost immediately. He walked on out to the truck and set the two small boxes on the front seat near the steering wheel.

He knew there were some rusted plow points and old tractor parts behind what had once been the family's garage. He had planned to sort through the junk and save what he could, but it wouldn't hurt to carry out a few pieces.

It was past ten o'clock when Walter arrived at the dumpsters. The sun had already climbed into a blinding arc. It was sultry, and the foul odor of the containers made him wince.

Walter climbed up into the bed of the truck and studied both dumpsters. Most of what he had thrown in last night had been picked through. The crumpled mattress lay in a different position. Walter assumed the little girl, or someone else, had tried to move it.

A plastic bag of garbage, glistening with noisy flies, had been poked open and searched for food. Any noble feeling Walter had had about what he was trying to do evaporated.

He shook his head. "This can't be! Not in our time. There are agencies to prevent this sort of thing," he assured himself.

He swallowed the dryness in his throat, turned around, and set about his task. He heaved into the nearest dumpster several tractor parts, one after the other. Each made a booming noise. He threw in an old plow point and listened to its loud ring.

"Surely, they will hear that," he mumbled aloud.

Then he climbed out of the truck's bed and returned to the cab for the groceries.

Where should he put them? He glanced about. He hadn't the faintest idea.

Momentarily, he set them down in the bed. He hoisted himself back into the truck and examined what appeared to be the cleaner of the two dumpsters.

There were five or six paint cans in the bottom, along with a plastic dropcloth and a gray mound of crushed sheetrock. He leaned forward, climbed out onto the lip of the dumpster, and lowered himself inside. He slipped on the sheetrock, lost his balance, and fell.

He struggled to sit up but just then heard a movement in the broom sedge above the embankment. It was the children!

"Shh, Davie!" whispered the little girl. "Git down!"

Walter lay very still and listened.

"I scared," whimpered the little boy.

"Shh!" repeated the older child. "I see a truck. Ain't nobody 'round. Wait here," she whispered. "An' don't move!"

Walter crouched as flat as he could against the sheetrock. What should he do if the little girl should discover him? He felt stupid. The last thing he wanted to do was to frighten her.

He held his breath, expecting her to find him any second. Instead, he heard her climb up onto the side of the truck.

"Davie!" she exclaimed. "He's throwin' food away! Git down here!" she whispered.

Walter exhaled quietly then drew a deep breath. The heat and tension had brought perspiration to his face. Flies crawled over his ears and mouth. He swatted silently at the pests. His legs ached with cramps.

"Davie, come on!" implored the little girl.

He listened as the tiny boy slid down the embankment. From the noise the children made, he could tell they were loading their arms up with food. He waited until he heard them struggle back up the clay bank. Finally, he smiled and pulled himself up.

Sweat coursed down his chin and neck. He could taste the chalky plaster of the sheetrock. It was all over his lips and face. His clothing was speckled white with it.

Walter looked around. The children were gone. What should he do? Follow them, reason dictated.

He wiped the plaster off the corners of his mouth and climbed out of the dumpster.

His legs cramped so that he hobbled the first few steps toward the embankment. With effort, he climbed it on all fours. When he reached the top, he crawled into the broom sedge, raised his head slowly, and looked about. No one was in sight.

About forty feet away grew a thin band of pines. Beyond and through them, he could see a clay gully or lane. It joined the main road farther down to his left. The remainder of the lane continued back through more pines and dropped out of sight beyond a depression.

He struggled to his feet and made his way through the tall grass to the pines and through them to the lane. He followed the lane until he came within sight of a dirt yard and a trailer on the edge of a clearing of white oaks and more pines.

The mobile home was dull maroon. He guessed it to be ten to twelve years old. It had settled on its concrete blocks and leaned unevenly to one side. A faded green Plymouth, with a low front tire, appeared to be stranded in the lane.

So that's where they lived.

Should he go on down and knock at their door? Or should he leave well enough alone?

He decided he should go to town. He would report the matter to the authorities and ask if he couldn't return with them. He would impress upon the sheriff, or whomever, a sense of urgency.

Walter retraced his steps to the truck. He was hot and grimy. He would have to go home, shower, and change clothes before he could go anywhere.

It was well past noon when Walter finally arrived at the courthouse. He parked his car by the curb, entered the old historic building, and proceeded down the hallway. He stopped outside the sheriff's office and glanced through the glass door. Lights were on, but no one was inside. He tried the door. It was locked.

"They ain't in right now," commented a young blonde. She was entering the clerk of the circuit court's office. "You ain't in trouble, are you?" she asked.

"No," he smiled. "I just want to report a family that needs help."

"What kind a help?" asked the girl. "They ain't been fightin', have they?"

"No," Walter replied. "They're poor, hungry. I think someone needs to go out and check on them."

"White or black?" she asked.

"White," he answered.

"They on food stamps?"

"I don't know," he said.

"Shoot, Mister. There's a lot a people that needs help in this county. White an' black. Sheriff already knows that. Why don't you report 'em to the DSS?"

"What's that?" he queried.

"Department of Social Services," she replied.

"They ain't in this buildin'. They're next to the library on South Main."

"Thank you," he nodded. "I know where that is."

"Good luck," she smiled, as she entered the office.

Walter strode uneasily out of the courthouse. He walked down to Pickens Street and turned left on South Main. He could see the sign from the corner where he was standing. He walked down to the office and entered.

A young black receptionist looked up from her desk. "May I help you?" she asked.

"Yes," said Walter. "I want to report a family out on old Mercy Road. They live in a trailer near some dumpsters. They appear to be destitute.

"I was disposing of some junk and garbage yesterday and came upon two children. Apparently they had been rummaging through the containers for food."

"O dear!" sighed the young receptionist. "That must be the Scruggs children. Whenever the old woman gets down, she can't get out, and the children go hungry. She's eligible for food stamps, but doesn't come in nearly as often as she could."

"Do you think anyone could go out and check on them?" Walter asked.

"I don't know," she replied. "Our staff has gone to Columbia today. They won't report back in until tomorrow. It may be two or three days before they can investigate."

"You will inform them, won't you, just as soon as they come in?" asked Walter.

"Oh, yes sir!" she assured him. "But it may be a day or two before they can get out there."

"Thank you," said Walter. "Good day," he added, as he turned and left the office.

Walter knew exactly what he had to do. He would return to the Mercy Road and go back to the mobile home. He would introduce himself to Mrs. Scruggs and ask how he might be of help.

He remembered that one of the car's tires was going flat. He decided that he ought to stop by the homeplace first, change clothes, put his jack and a spare tire in the back of the truck, and go out prepared to be of use.

The drive out to the dumpsters passed quickly. He drove just beyond the two containers and began looking for the lane. He spotted it, turned onto its furrowed ruts, and followed it back through the pines.

He beeped the horn as he came within sight of the trailer. The children were playing outside. His truck startled them, and they ran and clambered up into the trailer's entrance. They peered back at him from its door.

He stopped the truck, turned off its engine, and got out. "Hello!" he addressed the children. He tried to smile so as not to alarm them. "Can you tell me if Mrs. Scruggs is at home?"

The children scurried away from the door.

He approached the trailer with caution and paused at the entrance.

"Mrs. Scruggs? Mrs. Scruggs?" he called.

There was no answer.

"Mrs. Scruggs, are you at home?" he asked.

Still no answer.

He stepped up into the leaning trailer and glanced about.

A kitchen area, cluttered with cups and dishes and some of the food items he had brought to the dumpsters, was visible to his right. To his left ran a passageway. At the end of it he could see a den, and, beyond it, another passage and a bedroom.

He rapped on the side of the hallway. "Mrs. Scruggs, I'm one of your neighbors," he called. "Just come to check on you and the children. Are you all right?"

A sound in the kitchen startled him.

Suddenly, the little girl darted past him. The little boy followed her, ducked past her, and ran toward the rear of the trailer. The little girl stopped in the den and sat on the edge of a sofa.

Walter smiled and walked toward her. The little girl's eyes followed him. They were big with wonder and excitement.

"Granny's sick!" the little girl suddenly announced. "She can't hold her head up."

With that, she slipped off the sofa, held her hand up to Walter, and led him back toward the bedroom.

He ducked his head as he entered the room and nodded to the disabled woman in bed. She seemed addled and frightened at his appearance. The little boy crouched beside her.

"Hello, Mrs. Scruggs, how are you?" he asked.

Walter was about to speak again when he noticed an object on the woman's dresser. It caught his attention and compelled him to give it a second glance.

His mouth dropped open. It was a picture of himself and Ellen at the ball! It was the copy he had given Ellen forty-five years ago.

He looked again at the woman in the bed.

"Ellen? Are you Ellen?" he asked.

The woman tried to lift her head but could not.

Walter realized she had had a stroke.

He bent down and clasped the woman's left hand.

Her hair was gray and disheveled. Her neck was thin and pale. Time had filled her face with hardship and wrinkles. Her eyes searched his face and tried to focus on his mouth. Her lips trembled and strained to speak.

"Ellen!" Walter said. "O Ellen!" he whispered. "It is you!"

He knelt beside the bed and put his arm gently under her head. He cradled her face in his hands. Tears blurred his vision and his heart ached.

"Ellen! It's me, Walter. It's me," he said. "I've never stopped loving you," he whispered. "Never, in all these years."

She tried to raise her fingers to his lips but could not lift her arms. Her mouth quivered. She struggled to raise her head.

The little boy buried his face in his granny's pillow and wept. It was the pillow the little girl had salvaged from the dumpster.

The little girl clung to Walter and shuddered with fear.

Suddenly, a great sigh burst outward and upward from the woman. Her body jerked, relaxed, and slumped in his arms.

"Ellen! O Ellen!" Walter cried in a tiny voice. "Dear Ellen!" he moaned, as he rocked the woman in his arms.

Once more it is June.

The sun and sky are bright. A breeze stirs the woods in the bottom and rustles the cedar boughs on Mercy Hill.

Walter stands in the fescue near the boxwoods. He bends down and embraces the children who run toward him.

He hugs and kisses each child.

The wind picks up and stirs the limbs overhead. He glances into the sunlight, where it sparkles in the treetops.

"Run along, now," he whispers to the children, as he kisses the sparkles in their hair.

He watches the two run happily around the side of the house. Then he rises and returns to the porch. He pauses beside one of the columns and stares at the woods in the bottom and at the patch of ground just beyond them.

He cannot speak her name. But deep in his soul, his heart never ceases to repeat it.

And he remembers the land as it was when he was a child.

A PEOPLE WITH A STAR

A People with a Star

The November air was cold. Overhead, the late afternoon sky was blue, singed with a faint hue of bronze on the horizon. The orange radiance of the sun bathed the town's square and filled it with the waning light of day.

The merchant who had stepped outside his clothing store shivered in the shadows of the building and watched the workmen across the square. The men were lacing fresh cedar boughs into a wire-mesh frame constructed about the town's tall Confederate monument.

A man in a bucket-crane fastened a large white star atop the bough-graced monument. Then, with the help of companions below, he draped the tree with Christmas lights.

The merchant, Modein HaLevi, raised his cold hands to his lips, cupped them over his mouth, and warmed them with his breath.

How he loved this town, its proud Confederate marker, and the star atop the tree! He could claim all three. And it filled him with pride and joy and with a feeling he could not quite articulate.

Perhaps, if he had asked someone, they might have volunteered, "Humbleness." But it wasn't "humbleness." "Wonder," "awe," and "silence" were part of it, too. And something more complex that escaped his consciousness, that transcended him, and slipped off silently into the cold.

He felt at one with the square, at one with the monument, and at one with . . . "the Universe," he whispered. Although that wasn't it, either.

"Gearing up for the Christmas season, Modein?" teased a passerby. It was Devlin Wilson, a young lawyer.

"Me? Gear up?" replied the stocky, spectacled merchant. His breath had fogged over his glasses and his face glowed red with embarrassment. But he managed to retort, "Devlin, I have a new stock of Palmetto ties you need to see. And some fine leather belts, too!"

"Tomorrow," laughed the young lawyer. "Perhaps, tomorrow," he repeated, as he crossed the square toward the courthouse.

The merchant hugged his chilly forearms with his hands and returned inside his store. His glasses fogged up again and he removed them with a trembling hand—a nerve injury from World War II.

He paused beside his display window and wiped his glasses on a mannequin's sleeve. "Look, no one's watching!" he assured the mannequin. "I've been good to you. You've been good to me. That's been our arrangement for . . . how many years? Thirty-nine years! So that's not so bad," he smiled. He patted the mannequin's shoulder and slipped his spectacles back over his nose and ears.

He sighed. He rested his hands on the brass rail that separated the display window from the rest of his shop, and glanced out again across the square.

The workmen had completed their annual decoration of the monument. All was in place.

The bucket-seat had been lowered, and the foreman was testing the lights to see if they would illuminate properly. The star at the top glowed soft, clean, and pure with hope.

A tear suddenly stung the edge of Modein's right eye and trickled hot down his cheek. A droplet caught in his eyelash and blurred his vision.

Once more he removed his glasses. He crouched momentarily behind the mannequin, in the hope that no one outside had seen him.

As he wiped his eye dry, a fantasm of old memories, faces, and images crept onto the stage of his heart and waited to be acknowledged.

"Polly, Polly," he whispered. But Polly, his wife of thirty-five years, was dead. "Not dead," he countered to himself. "Not dead to me, only gone . . . ," his voice whistled in a whisper that only God and his soul could hear.

"Ah!" he groaned with disgust, as he shrugged his shoulders and forced himself to strike a more optimistic pose. He resettled his glasses over his nose and peered out again at the square.

Indeed, his soul belonged to this town. It had been his dwelling place throughout his generation. It had been his family's home since the burning of Columbia.

Like the patriarch of old, his great-grandfather had come to a land of promise, and ultimately to this town, and here had found land, family, blessing, and a name.

Exactly how far back the family could trace its lineage was debatable. Modein had never thought of himself as a devout Jew, but the name HaLevi had often made him wonder if his ancestors might not have been Levites, or at least Israelites, whose roots were traceable to Solomon's time.

"And why not?" Modein wondered aloud. "The name says it all."

But why stop with Solomon? he mused. For couldn't his ancestors have also gone up with Samuel to Gilgal, or fought beside Joshua when they captured Ai, or wandered with Moses in the wilderness, and possibly, just possibly, have beheld Mount Sinai, or have huddled that night with that frightened rabble by the bay, when that strong east wind blew out of the Sinai and drove back that long, dark wall of waves?

Yet, it was one of those fantasies he could not share with everyone. His closest gentile friends would laugh at him if they knew. "Imagine! Modein actually believes his bloodline is that pure!"

No. Some things one can only whisper to oneself, or, at best, share with one's spouse or children, as on the evenings of Passover and Yom Kippur. And then, only at table with family, or in the somber lamplight of a synagogue.

Napoleon. His sister had insisted, to the night of her death, that, historically, their lineage was traceable to the Napoleonic era. But beyond that she would not conjecture.

She had written as much in an unpublished genealogy. She had based it on an old German trunk full of diaries, letters, newspaper clippings, and wedding and dowry records that went back to the 1830s. She had also consulted histories, biographies, and synagogue registers, "and injected an inordinate amount of Jewish *chutzpah,*" he used to tease her.

"And what if I did?" she would cough, as she struggled to retain her good humor, though the tubercular hand of death had pallored her countenance. "It's true, Modie. It's all true," she would wheeze. "The letters in the trunk are irrefutable."

"But Rosa," he would argue, "they're all in Yiddish. And grandfather Abib was the last Jew in our family to read and write Yiddish."

"Not so!" she would rebut. "He taught me how to read Yiddish, so someone could remember."

"But you were only a child when he died."

"I was thirteen!" she gasped.

"Now, Modie, don't be so hard on Rosa," Polly would chide him. She would lean forward in her chair and put her soft hands firmly on his. Her almond-shaped eyes would glare at him beseechingly, then overflow with pity, patience, and love.

"It's true," Rosa would whisper. "Even the part about great-grandfather Samuel's father seeing Napoleon, and his brother later seeing Czar Alexander when the czar toured Poland.

"That's what inspired Samuel to yearn to be free. Free like the czar! Free to travel! Free to leave Poland! And free to be a Jew!" she would choke.

"Can't you imagine how it must have been!" she would exclaim. "The Napoleonic Wars were over. The Congress of Vienna had convened, drafted its treaty, and dissolved. Czar Alexander the First had promised freedom to the Poles. Never had hope burned brighter in their hearts! Then came the Uprising of 1830 and Czar Nicholas the First's avowal to destroy the Polish nationality and language forever. Universities were closed. The young men were conscripted into the army. And thousands of Polish families were exiled to Siberia."

"But what has that to do with the HaLevis?" he would interrupt her.

"Everything!" she would gasp, tears glistening in her eyes. "In England, Queen Victoria had ascended the throne. Belgium had secured its independence from Holland. The Greeks were rebelling against the Turks. And Charles the Tenth's rule had ended in France.

"Modein, it was the year 1835. And in our ancestral village of Suwalka, Poland, Samuel HaLevi was being married to Leah Ruth Wynesky.

"Think of it, Modein. They were only sixteen. But they shared all the hopes and dreams of that turbulent period. That's the connection!" she would cough.

"Rosa, you must rest," Polly would insist. "How do you keep it up, when you are so ill?"

"Strength. It gives me strength, Polly. To reach back to those young Polish lovers and to read those old Yiddish letters and records gives me strength. That's how."

Modein realized that he was tugging on the brass rail and that his right arm was trembling. He reached up and momentarily grasped the mannequin for support.

A customer had entered the store. It was Mrs. Wheeler, Mrs. Harriet Able Wheeler. Her house on North Main had the distinction of quartering some of the officers who had accompanied President Davis to Abbeville and who had later escorted him across the Savannah.

"Mrs. Wheeler, you honor this daydreaming merchant with your presence," he smiled.

"Oh, Mr. HaLevi," she laughed. "I just want to see your Palmetto ties. Devlin Wilson tells me you have a brand new supply in stock. And guess who intends to select the best first?"

"They're right here," he motioned, as he accompanied her to the rack. "Please have a good look. And remember, the limit is ten!" he added somberly.

"Oh, Mr. HaLevi!" she laughed.

Modein grinned and laughed with her.

He watched her pull out half-a-dozen and stroke them before she chose two. "Now don't tell Laurie what I've done, or you'll spoil it all," she scolded him. Then she smiled and asked if he would gift-wrap them.

"My pleasure," he replied. But actually he thought to himself, "You've been good to me. I've been good to you. It's a nice arrangement, isn't it, Mrs. Wheeler?" He smiled.

After she left, he returned to the display window and rejoined his silent partner by the rail.

It was almost dark outside. The workmen had long since vacated the square. The street lamps were beginning to blink on.

Fate had been kind to him and to his family, he knew. He marveled that Samuel HaLevi had ever made it out of Poland. And he knew where he, Modein, would be today, if Samuel had not longed for freedom and travel. He would be lying in a mass grave, with thousands of nameless Jews, sacrificed on the altar of the Nazi Molech.

Instead he was here, staring out at this town, staring out at this square, and staring out at its monument that he loved.

Yes, it was more than "awe," or "wonder," or "silence." It was something he didn't articulate to himself anymore, though he lived with its presence and felt it in his soul. It was more than the "universe." More than the "universal." Though it slipped away into the Void whenever he stopped and thought about it, as he was doing now.

He patted the mannequin on its shoulder and sighed. His mind wandered again. . . .

"They were so young, Modein," Rosa was saying.

"Think of it, Polly, what it would be like if Modein had left you in that tiny Polish village, along with two infants, to seek his fortune in England?"

"I should have been terrified," replied Polly. "I would have cried my life out a little each day."

"And don't you know that Leah Ruth must have done the same?" coughed Rosa. "But things went well for Samuel, for those English cousins of ours helped him gain those business skills he needed before coming here.

"Imagine, after only three years in London, he set sail from Liverpool and arrived in Charleston in the summer of 1842." A sense of personal fulfillment glowed on Rosa's face. "Then, with the financial backing of his cousins, he purchased that jewelry business we all still talk about!" She began to cough and wheeze again. . . .

Another customer had come into the store.

"Staying open a bit late, aren't you?" commented the curious shopper.

Modein recognized him as a professor at Ebenezer College in nearby DeWitt. "I'm Modein HaLevi," he said, offering him his hand. "Aren't you a professor at Ebenezer?"

"Yes," replied the tall, portly bald man, as he shook Modein's hand. "I'm Edgar Hubbard. I teach in the Humanities Department, namely, courses in philosophy, art, and history. I've only been here two years, but I love your town and I love your square."

"My sentiments, too," Modein concurred. "I was just standing here by the window, admiring the tree and the monument out there in the dark.

"I don't mean to appear vain," Modein said, "but my grandfather contributed to the raising of that monument. He did it in memory of his oldest brother, who was killed at Petersburg. He was a member of Orr's Regiment of Rifles."

"I've heard of them," acknowledged the professor. "What a valiant lot they must have been! What was it? Three thousand of them left from this area, and only three hundred returned?"

Both men shook their heads, as if still stunned by the magnitude and horror of that tragedy.

"You know," Modein boasted with a smile, "my great-grandfather, Samuel HaLevi, used to live in DeWitt. He moved there from Charleston in the early 1850s to get away from the heat and yellow fever. He even helped the professors with their Hebrew at the Divinity School there. He's the one who designed the Hebrew seal over the entranceway to the Towers building."

"How fascinating!" exclaimed Hubbard. "Please, go on."

Modein was tired, and he knew it was late, but he needed to talk to this stranger. Something deep within him was seeking to express itself. Reaching out for someone, somewhere, who would listen and understand.

"In the 1850s my great-grandfather owned a sizable plantation near DeWitt, but toward the close of the war, he moved his family down to Columbia, thinking they would be safer there than either here or in Charleston."

"How ironic!" smiled the professor.

"Ah," sighed Modein. "The Yankees burned him out, anyway. The story is that on the night Columbia was burned, the HaLevi family was seated around the *Shabbat* meal. The *Shabbat* candles were burning in their silver stands in the center of the table. And the table was spread with a fresh cloth and set with china and silver.

"Suddenly, a sharp rap at the door brought apprehension to them all. My great-grandfather rose, went to the door, where a Yankee major politely introduced himself. The officer said he regretted it, but that he had orders to search the premises, free any slaves the family had, and confiscate whatever the army might need.

"The wise Samuel HaLevi agreed, but first insisted that the officer join the family at the table, as the *Shabbat* could not be dishonored by them.

"At this, the two rejoined the others at table, enjoyed the evening meal, and observed the *Shabbat*.

"The servants came in, cleared away the china and most of the silver and placed the *Shabbat* candleholders on a buffet.

"Samuel was about to offer the major a cigar when the officer rose and cleared his throat. 'I deeply regret this,' he said, 'but my men have been waiting outside. I must let them in now to pillage your house, as those are our orders.'

"With that, one of the servants—a beloved mammy—suddenly entered the room, seized the tablecloth in her hands, and whisked the remaining silver away!

"The Yankees went on to pillage the house. They stole the *Shabbat* candleholders and burned my great-grandfather's house to the ground. But the mammy, who had taken the tablecloth, had run outside in the yard. There she tucked the tablecloth under her skirts, gathered the children around her, and fell in a grieving position upon the ground.

"My family still has a few pieces of the silver," sighed Modein. "As for the candleholders, my great-grandfather had a duplicate set cast. They were in bronze. One is lost, but the other is as dear to our family as any two could be. I keep it in an old German chest," smiled Modein, "in a sort of hideaway place."

"I can't believe that, but I do," asserted the surprised and deeply moved professor.

The man glanced suddenly at his watch. "My goodness!" he exclaimed. "It's past seven. I must be somewhere else. I'll come back again," he promised.

"Please do," intoned Modein. "I'll be good to you. And your shopping here will be good for me. It's an arrangement that never fails."

The professor smiled. "*Shalom!* And a blessed *Shabbat* to you!" he called, as he turned and waved good night.

The words, "*Shabbat* to you," suddenly jolted Modein. He hadn't expected that. And, indeed, it was the sabbath. The Jewish sabbath! Which he hadn't observed since Polly's death. His mouth fell open, and he moved to the window and stared out into the night.

The street lights filled the square with their lambent glow. He looked up at the tree. It loomed tall and dark where it shrouded the monument, for it would not be lighted officially until next week. Nevertheless, the shimmer of the square's lights illumined the pale star atop the tree.

Polly had made the star herself, and its six points were clearly visible. They had given it to the city one Thanksgiving, just before Hanukkah.

Tears filled Modein's heart and welled up into his eyes and coursed freely down his face and cheeks.

Suddenly, Modein locked the door, turned off the shop's lights, and hurried quickly to the back of his store. There, in a secluded corner of a storeroom, under a table of spare merchandise, he knelt down and slid forward a heavy object. It was the old German chest.

Its humped lid was covered with dust and was gray with fuzz and lint. He wiped off the corners of the chest and raised the great lid.

There, piled in tied bundles in the bottom of the chest, were Samuel HaLevi's letters in Yiddish to his beloved Leah Ruth, which she had brought with her from Poland and Bremen. And, precisely where he had wrapped and laid it six years ago, was the bronze *Shabbat* candleholder.

He bent down and spread his hands out upon the old brown letters. The faded ink was barely visible, but he was reaching far past the scrawled lettering and brittle pages.

He pressed his fingertips down upon the bundles for a long time. Then he unwrapped the candleholder and raised it to his bosom. He clutched it with all the strength his trembling right arm would allow. Then he sank to his side on the floor.

"Jew. I'm a Jew!" he whispered. "I'm a Jew."

Or was he saying, "You, is it You? Is it You?"

A visitor, hidden in the room, could not have determined the difference.

Whichever it was, the silence enveloped him. The ineffable closed round Modein. And the tighter he clasped the candleholder, the tighter he felt grasped. . . . "Yes, yes!" he whispered, by something eternal, something divine.

Then he did something, whispered something, he hadn't whispered for years.

"Shema Yisraeil: Adonai Eloheinu, Adonai Echad!"

"Hear, O Israel: The Lord our God is one Lord!"

Note: Portions of Rosa's reminiscences were inspired by a reading of *The Winstocks of South Carolina,* by Evelyn R. Gross (Compiled in Greenwood, S.C., 1961–62).

BLACKBERRY WINTER

Blackberry Winter

The March landscape lay brown and dormant, though the worst of winter had passed. Tan stalks of dried Johnson grass and other weeds hugged the clay gullies and crept back through the undergrowth toward the edge of the pine forest in the distance.

Miz Pearl—Mrs. Pearlene Goodman by marriage—stood on the narrow front porch of her tiny, three-room farmhouse and looked down the gravel road. An old Dodge had pulled up in the drive of the only house within sight of hers.

Nettie Jordan had died two months earlier. Nettie had been Pearlene's closest neighbor. She and Nettie had known each other since the Depression, when their husbands had journeyed downstate to work for the CCC's.

Now someone else was renting Nettie's place.

Pearlene was pleased to have neighbors again, but she was apprehensive at the same time.

None but the poorest families would have to live as far from a main road as she. She wondered what plight or destitution had befallen her neighbors-to-be; or if not destitution, how coarse and roughneck they might prove to be.

Deer poachers, drifters, alcoholics, drug dealers, and even a house break-in ring were known to ply the county's back roads. Hers was certainly no exception. She had seen too many strange cars and scurfy-looking men to suppose otherwise.

She pulled her shawl about her shoulders and stepped out into the sunshine. The dried thatchlike branches of a dead chinaberry tree cast their spidery shadow across the porch.

The tree had died eight years ago, but she had been unable to find anyone to cut it down. She could remember, though, when its shade was a welcome relief from the sun and when it was one of the few trees in sight of what was otherwise an endless patchwork of bustling farms, dotted white with thousands of bursting cotton bolls.

Now the land was bleak. Its fields had not been plowed in years, and many had been abandoned to erosion, broom sedge, and cedars, or were overgrown with sumac, spiny oaks, pines, and gum trees.

Only one phenomenon broke the dreary scene around Miz Pearl's farmhouse. That was the incredible sight of the banks of blackberry bushes that blossomed along both sides of the road.

The tall plants were profuse with white blooms and stretched all the way down the fencerow between her place and Nettie's. They looked like long hay rows, powdered white with snow.

"Blackberry winter," her father had called it. "A time when Nature longs for spring and sneaks past the frost, only to have it grow cold again."

Her father had died in 1923, the same year in which she had met Jim, her husband.

As she stood there and stared down the fencerow, it was impossible not to think of both men.

Her father had loved blackberries. Blackberry pies. Blackberry jelly. Blackberry anything.

The wisest statement she had ever heard had come from his lips.

At the time, she was a child of nine. It was late May or early June, and they were picking berries along the road.

It was hot and the briars were scratching her tiny arms. She had crawled under the bushes, where the soil was dank and the air redolent of berries.

There in the shade, she could glance up through the vines at the big ripe berries. They looked so easy to pick. But each time she reached up to pull one, the motion knocked other fat berries to the ground. She had begun to fuss and cry.

Her father heard her and came over where she was. He peered through the briars to observe her.

Just then she knocked off more berries. She winced and wiped back her sweat and tears.

"Hun," he smiled, "some things are inevitable." Then he wandered on down the row.

If she were only able, she would visit his grave and lay a bouquet of berry vines beside the marker.

Poor Jim! She needed to visit his grave, too. It hadn't been cleaned off since last Memorial Day. But with Nettie dead, she hated to impose too often on the church folk who looked after her.

She stared again toward Nettie's. She had been inside when the car had pulled up, and she was eager to catch a glimpse of her new neighbors, or whoever they were.

Her big calico cat had come around from the back of the house and was rubbing against her leg. It purred and waited for her to bend down and stroke it.

"Khaki! Go on!" said Miz Pearl. "I don't have time for you. I'm too worried," she said.

But with that, she bent down and picked up the heavy cat.

"My, but you're a fatty," said Pearlene, as she rubbed the cat affectionately.

"You're all I've got," she sighed. "But you keep the rats away."

She stroked the cat and carried it back toward the rear of the house.

She set it down on the back steps and walked up the path toward her garden. She counted its remaining winter collard plants. "Seven," she said aloud to herself.

It was time to have the garden plowed again. But that meant she'd have to ask someone and then wait around until they could squeeze it in.

She turned and studied Nettie's place again. No one had come out of the house or had returned to the car. She guessed they didn't have any children or she would have seen them by now.

Maybe it was only someone checking on the property. She hoped not. She'd been so lonely since Nettie's death.

The sun was warm and a gentle breeze stirred the dry grass all around her.

She walked up the path toward an old pigpen. The lot was overgrown with polk berry stalks, briars, and low-growing honeysuckle. The honeysuckle leaves were both green and bright red.

She hadn't raised any pigs in over twelve years. She had thought of having the lot plowed up. But she hated to see the old pens and troughs go.

It was here, sixty-one years ago, that she had met Jim. He was a boy of fourteen, she a girl of eleven. He had come over with his father from a neighboring farm. The two had walked over to drive home a gang of pigs.

Jim's father had had to sell his place and had become a tenant for another man. Pearlene's father had felt sorry for him and had given him and his family the pigs.

Jim was a gangly, tall boy, with a wild shock of hair standing straight up over his left brow. His blue overalls had faded gray. He was barefooted and was keeping his distance from the pigs.

"Come on, boy, an' gang 'em up!" his father had called to him.

Jim blushed and hurried along to keep up with the pigs.

Pearlene waved to him and smiled. She followed him down the lane to the road.

At the road, Jim looked back, smiled, and waved to her. From that moment on, they fell in love. They married four years later.

No. She would keep the old pigpen. There was no need to do away with it now.

She turned and walked back down the path.

Blackberries were in bloom all the way back across her land, to the very edge of the woods.

She remembered the night her father had pleaded with the sheriff's posse not to lynch a young Negro who had "attacked" a white girl.

"No, sir!" the deputy had shaken his head. "He done made advances on her. He done tore off her clothes. These men know whut to do. You jus' git on back to the house. Me an' these men'll take care of this nigger."

Her father was very angry but knew he had lost. She had run out in the field to him. She was crying and scared.

He bent down and put his arm around her. "Come on, honey," he whispered. There were tears in his eyes. Then he picked her up and carried her back to the house.

The next morning, smoke drifted low in the woods and over the fields. The air was still and reeked of gun powder and singed hair.

It was a corner of her childhood she could never forget. And it reminded her of a similar incident, which had occurred in the early forties.

She had been picking berries along the road when she heard a rustling in the bushes. At first she thought it was a rabbit, or perhaps some birds. But when neither darted out, she became frightened.

She realized it might be a snake. And she was afraid to step forward or back.

With caution, she parted several vines and peered into the musty shadows of the bushes.

She heard the movement again. It was to her right, deep in the bushes.

To her horror, she saw a foot and then the crouched form of a man. She started to scream, until she realized she was staring into the frightened eyes of a young boy.

He was dressed in prison garb. His hands and face were scratched and bleeding. He was an escapee from the chain gang!

"Please, ma'am, don't tell on me," he said. "I ain't gonna hurt you. I ain't done nothin' bad."

"Who are you?" she asked.

"I'm Billy Iva's boy, from over at Level Land. Me an' some boys was caught stealin' cigarettes. That's all, ma'am. Please don't turn me in. I got some cousins over in Georgia. I was jus' tryin' to git there."

She glanced again at Nettie's place. She and Nettie had hid the boy that day, given him some clean clothes, and had fed him supper before he slipped away toward Calhoun Falls that evening.

Pearlene had buried his jail suit. She was standing not more than ten feet from the spot. She guessed his clothing had long since rotted.

She walked on back to the house and returned to the front porch.

She stared again at Nettie's.

She was about to enter her house when she saw Nettie's screen door open and a bearded man in a denim jacket step out. He was tall and quite large.

Oh, no! her heart sank. "A hippie!" she muttered aloud.

She hurried to the door and entered. She went quickly to her living room window and peered out behind the curtains.

The man had ambled out into the road and was walking up toward her place. He stopped midway along the road and waved to her.

She stepped back from the curtains. How dare him! Who did he think he was?

She peered out again. He was almost in her yard. She hurried to the door and opened it.

"Who are you?" she shouted. "Don't you come no closer."

The big man stopped. He was on the edge of her property. He wiped the sweat off his forehead and glanced up at the dead chinaberry tree.

"Miz Pearl, I'll see that you git a new tree here, ma'am," he smiled.

"How do you know my name?" she called.

"I've knowed you a long time, Miz Pearl," he said. "I don't mean to frighten you none."

"Who are you?"

"I know you don't know me," he said, "but," he continued, as he walked closer, "you he'ped my older brother onced, 'long time ago. Jimmy Iva. Remember? I'm Gerald, his brother. I'm goin' to be your new neighbor. An' any time you ever need me, I'll be right here."

"O Mr. Iva!" cried Pearlene. "I am surprised! And so obliged!"

She smiled and hurried out into the yard and hugged the big man.

THE OPTIMIST

The Optimist

The tall, willowy, black principal dreaded the coming confrontation. Now it would soon occur.

"That white boy's daddy's goin' to bust you," warned Willie. "He ain't gonna take no sweet talk off o' you. Ma'k my wo'ds, Mr. Greene. Yes-suh!"

Willie was the school's janitor. He was sixty, gentle, and big.

"Thank you, Mr. Oley," said the principal. "But we owe him the chance to be reasonable. We'll see."

"Well, I' be down the hall, if you needs me," Willie volunteered.

Greene appreciated Willie. But he was confident he could handle Bobby's father. It wasn't the first time he had been threatened by an angry parent.

Fortunately, race was not the central issue. He thanked God for that. Besides, the decision to transfer Bobby to Columbia hadn't been his, but the court's. Mr. Lanch would surely see that, he hoped.

He glanced at his watch and walked back to his office.

Would that Bobby's father had the attitude that the black child's grandmother had evinced. But he couldn't expect a white man to fathom that solemn sense of resignation, so characteristic of his people.

"That Fontaine!" she had bewailed. "He has grieved me till I is gray. I s'pose God knows bes'," she sighed. "I done did my part, Mr. Greene. Let him dance to his own tune!"

Back in his office, Greene picked up the boys' folders, which his secretary had placed on his desk, and sat down. He glanced through their records, one more time.

Both were in the eighth grade. Each had failed a lower grade, or, at some point, had been held back a year.

Test scores indicated that the white youth was reading on a

fourth-grade level, the black child on a third. They were ranked in the lowest national percentiles in all categories.

He shook his head somberly. Hardly auspicious statistics. Moreover, the incident that had erupted between the two boys forecast a chilling future.

The boys had drawn knives on each other in the lunch line. Bobby had been drinking wine, stolen from the Pantry. Fontaine was high on drugs.

Each had cut the other so badly that both had been hospitalized. Fontaine was at home. Bobby was in the Abbeville jail, waiting to be sent to Columbia. He had stabbed a teacher, a coach, and the arresting officer.

Greene closed the folders and pushed them back. He felt a sickness in the pit of his stomach.

It was the twentieth century, he assured himself. In fact, the last quarter of the twentieth century. Yet illiteracy and poverty were everywhere.

Poor South Carolina! Still at the bottom of every national educational study, every column, and every norm. When would the legislators stop defying the governor's efforts to lift the state from the bottom?

"Gracious God Almighty!" he groaned. "When?"

There was a rap at his door. "Yes?" he called.

It was Mrs. Horne, the school's secretary. She was a small, nervous, middle-aged woman. Her black hair was dyed entirely too black. A grim expression belied her own anxiety. Her thin lips accentuated the pallor of her face.

"It's three-thirty, Mr. Greene," she said, with a jejune stare. "He should be here soon."

"I know," he replied. "I expect him around four."

"Shouldn't I phone the police?"

"I've thought about that," he answered, rising to his feet. He flexed his long slender fingers and pressed them against the desk. "I don't think so. It would only exacerbate matters, I believe."

He rocked forward on his fingertips, then relaxed his hands.

"This is a schoolhouse," he reflected aloud. "I *am* its principal," he smiled. "I must reason with him. Not accost him with threats and police. Or else, we are not in the educating business, but in the

. . . intimidating business. And we do too much of that already," he frowned.

"You don't know Bobby's father," she replied. "The boy comes from a violent family. His uncle killed a man last spring, but the jury was afraid to find him guilty. Bobby's mother beat up a deputy at the Jockey Lot only last week."

"I've heard," he said pensively. "I plan to stay out of his way and not provoke him. Thank you for your concern."

He glanced at his watch. "You've put in a full day, Mrs. Horne. Please feel free to leave anytime. It might be best if Mr. Lanch and I met alone."

A smile of incredulity appeared momentarily on her lips. "Thank you for offering," she said, "but I'll remain for awhile. I have a few stencils I need to type."

He nodded respectfully in appreciation as she closed the door.

"Gracious God!" he mumbled to himself. "I wish he would come on."

Greene walked about his desk and picked up the metal paperweight he had acquired during his college days. It was the Philosophy Award. He had been the recipient his senior year.

It was a handsome medallion, made of burnished bronze or some kind of brass alloy. He didn't know which. It gleamed in the light as he turned it slowly with his fingers.

He angled it away from the glare and read its inscription:

Robert Quenton Greene
May 27, 1951
Philosophy Award
"The unexamined life is
unworthy of a man."
ἀλήθεια, ἀγαθόν, καλόν

"Truth, goodness, and beauty," he whispered to himself, as he translated the Greek words on the medallion.

He admired the ancient Greeks. They believed that truth and virtue were inseparable. Bring one to the truth and one should want to do good.

Of course, not all learning is in order to do goodness, he knew. But he concurred essentially with the Greeks.

Wasn't public education founded on such a hope? On such a vision?

But, he reflected, if schools are continually denied adequate funding, competent and dedicated teachers, and all they require; and if, especially in the poorer counties, such as his, they are denied teacher's aids, remedial classes, and parents who care, then how can a child from an illiterate home ever be brought to the truth and to virtue and to beauty?

Wasn't it all an illusive and deceptive hoax?

Yet, what was its alternative?

He shook his head sideways, then set his jaw, and nodded affirmatively. He returned the paperweight to his desk.

Education was his people's only hope. As well as the illiterate white man's. Of that, he was confident.

Hadn't the state forfeited the birthrights of far too many Bobbys and Fontaines already? And for what?

"Kind God Almighty, for what?"

He sighed and sat down at his desk. He picked up a letter opener and fumbled with it. His mind wandered.

He remembered the schoolhouse he had attended as a child. All black in those days. The sixth, seventh, and eighth grades had met in the same room. He had taught himself, for the most part. His own teacher had enlisted him to teach the slower children.

Sometimes in the afternoon he read them stories. He had the privilege of selecting what he read. Sometimes he read from the Bible. Sometimes from Shakespeare. *Othello* and *Julius Caesar* were still his favorites.

He had studied journalism in college and had wanted to be a writer. But no newspaper would hire him.

That had hurt deeply at the time. Still, public education was a worthy calling, he allowed. It would pass the Almighty's tribunal, where truth and goodness and beauty are seated at the right hand of wisdom and joy.

He laid the letter opener along the edge of his blotter.

Fumbling with it had brought to memory the letter his mother had written him before her death. He had not received it until after the funeral.

He had discovered it on returning to work. Tears had come to his eyes upon recognizing her handwriting.

He had carried it into his office and had opened it first. His hands had trembled then, as they were now.

He had made a copy of the letter, taken the original home, and had filed the copy in a special folder marked "Mama."

He smiled, pushed back his chair, and walked over to the file cabinet. He had not read her letter in months.

He wondered how she had done it. She had reared eleven children, nine of whom were still living.

In his mind, he could still visualize the tiny, three-room tenant house, near Antreville, where his mother had given birth to him at the height of the Depression. Though he knew that tiny dwelling was now used for storing hay, he would always think of it as "home."

There, in its whitewashed rooms, he had grown up as a child. All thirteen of them had slept in two rooms. Most of the sweet potatoes, greens, and cornbread they ever had to eat they had raised themselves. And there, along the clay ridges and troughs of the Clagden farm, they had plowed, "chopped," and picked cotton, well up into the late 1940s.

He was the last of his mama's children—her baby. The summer after his birth, his father was kicked to death by a mule. The family had no place to go, so continued to work for the Clagdens.

Then, as the years past, his mother began taking in washing and ironing, in order to help him go to school. He was the only one of the eleven to receive a "formal education."

His mama could barely write. But she was a wise and persistent woman. "No" was simply not a word in her metaphysical inventory.

He pulled out the folder, opened it, and took out her letter.

Deer Robert,

I is bad off. Goin to die.

You is the baby. You can hep the others. You been to school. You is de edugated one. The god above is always look down haplieе on you.

Times is changed. Always blieve in the good god, yoself, and others. An blieve in de wites. De wites is goin to change to.

Don't hate no body.
Don't reevange yoself.
Have paytions with yo sistuhs an brothuhs.
God will take care of you.
Love always.
Mama

He held her letter thoughtfully for a long while.

Times had certainly changed. And changed again. That was true. For since the 1950s, he had witnessed two great changes, as far as his race was concerned.

One had come in the sixties, with civil rights and integration. It had been a time of freedom and liberation, a time of progress and jubilation. It was the black man's giant step forward, for all mankind.

But the second had come in the seventies and had yet to complete its course. It was a strange, yet understandable, time.

It was a time of black pride and black achievement. Yet a time of deep hatred and alienation.

It was a time of undisciplined indulgence and of wallowing in ignorance. A time jaded by the loss of self-esteem and marked by increased welfarism.

It was a time of new bondage and degradation for blacks everywhere. It was the black man's sad step backward, for all mankind.

He returned his mother's letter to the folder, refiled it, and closed the cabinet drawer.

He walked to the window and stared out across the parking lot. The September sunshine glossed the asphalt with a brilliant sheen. Perhaps it was a good omen. "Hail, Apollo," he whispered. "Are you there?"

He smiled and put his fingertips up against the windowpanes, as if to catch the light.

His own role in the civil rights movement had been a modest one. But he had welcomed the challenge for responsible involvement, which the striking down of the old segregation codes had made possible. He knew that most of his generation shared that enthusiasm, too.

But what had happened since the sixties?

Today's children of integration seemed so less motivated, so less ambitious than the children of those segregation years.

The one group had hungered for education, for opportunities, for involvement as equals in the great democracy that had finally yielded up its treasures of rights and liberties to their just and righteous crusade.

But the children of integration seemed so hostile, so determined to abuse those very principles of democracy and freedom that could make them whole.

Indeed, the grandparents of the children in his school were more concerned for their grandchildren's education than were the children's own parents. Most of those grandparents were even more articulate, self-reliant, and proud of their hard-earned opportunities than were the parents of the children in his school.

"Gracious God," he thought, "we are still wandering in the wilderness, burdened down by the baggage of our own prejudice and despair."

New wine cannot be poured into old wine skins. How true!

Yet it was hardly that simple.

Most of those parents worked the second shift at the mills, thus necessitating their absence from home at the hours when their children most needed their presence.

Moreover, he wondered how genuinely whites had accepted integration. Sometimes their vacant stares and indifferent glances aroused within him a dimension of isolation he could not dispel.

And how easily old wounds were reopened by that singular epithet that his soul would forever deplore!

He had gone to the PTO meeting to encourage parents to support the school's need for remedial classes, when the little white girl had pointed at him and whispered that epithet for all to hear. It caught him totally by surprise and destroyed his sense of dignity.

He took a deep breath and put his hands in his pockets.

He wished Lanch would come on. But what should he say to him? That Bobby was only a mirror of the pit of illiteracy that held them all in its grasp? That white and black together, they were doomed to drown in its sea? That there was nothing they could do to challenge or to change their fate?

"No, no!" he uttered. "I will not bow before that tempting altar!"

He was about to return to his desk when he saw Lanch's pickup truck swing slowly into the asphalt lot and park in the space next to his own car.

He had met Bobby's father several times before. He thought he knew about what to expect.

He watched the big man open the door and get out. He seemed larger and more menacing than Greene had remembered him.

His hair was cropped close to his head. He wore a faded, blue work shirt, rolled up at the sleeves, and a pair of low-fitting khaki trousers. His stomach protruded over his belt, and his massive chest filled his shirt smooth. He seemed to favor his right leg as he walked impatiently toward the school's entrance.

Greene expelled a deep sigh and moved toward his desk. He placed Bobby's folder on the blotter and sat down.

What was he going to say?

That would depend on Mr. Lanch, he supposed.

He could hear the big man enter the outside office. Muffled vibrations of the man's husky voice left no doubts as to his presence.

The knock at his door caused Greene physically to jerk.

"Yes, Mrs. Horne!" he answered.

She opened the door. "Mr. Lanch is here to see you," she said nervously, as the big man stepped ominously into the room.

Greene looked apprehensively at Mrs. Horne.

"Thank you, come in," he said, all in the same breath.

He indicated for Mrs. Horne to close the door and to leave them in privacy.

He leaned quickly across the desk to shake Mr. Lanch's hand.

The big man had not expected this gesture and shook Greene's hand with a surprised lifelessness.

Before Lanch could speak, Greene seized the initiative.

"Please be seated, Mr. Lanch. I'm so glad you have come. There's a great deal we need to talk about. Perhaps together we can help Bobby."

"I ain't inter'stid in no talkin'," grunted Bobby's father. "An' I ain't inter'stid in sittin' in no cheer with you. In fact, I ain't inter'stid in me and you doin' *nothin'* together."

The big man leaned forward and put his hands on Greene's desk. He looked him squarely in the eyes. "I come to call you a liar! An' I'm goin' to drag you to Abb'ville an' make you re-test-tify whut you seen!

"That nigger boy drawed his knife first. My boy wont doin' nothin' but protectin' hisself."

"You know I can't retestify," replied Greene.

"Then I'll bust you right here and now!" grimaced Lanch.

"Mr. Lanch, sit down, please! I have Bobby's folder. You need to see what's inside and understand what it means."

"The onliest thing I und'erstan' is that you put in it, whutever's in there. An' I ain't inter'stid in that."

Greene picked up the folder. "Please, let us be reasonable!"

"Give me that damn thing!" ordered Lanch, as he grabbed the folder out of Greene's hands and flung it toward the window.

"Now you come here," demanded Lanch. "I'm goin' to collar you good."

With that, Lanch lunged for the tall, gentlemanly Negro. He seized him by the shoulders and, in one powerful motion, lifted him off the floor and dragged him onto the desk. In the process, the big man lost his balance and fell to his knees in front of the desk. He was still holding on to Greene's coat.

Greene floundered about, groping for support. Suddenly, his right hand found a heavy object to which he could cling. It was the paperweight.

He clasped it tightly in his hand and raised his arm to strike Lanch. Just as he was about to bring his arm forward, his fingertips pressed against the raised letters of those Greek words he cherished: *ἀλήθεια, ἀγαθόν, καλόν*. Truth, goodness, beauty.

Tears filled Greene's eyes, wild now with desperation and shock. "Gracious God Almighty!" he growled.

Lanch looked up at that transfigured face of agony and let go.

"Whut have I done?" groaned Lanch, as he rolled back on the floor to dodge the paperweight, which Greene still clasped in his hand.

Both men stared at each other. They could hear Willie in the outside office. "Mr. Greene, Mr. Greene! Ah you all right?"

Lanch slowly struggled to his feet, while Greene regained his composure and eased back into his chair.

"Yes, Willie! I'm all right," called the principal.

Neither Lanch nor Greene spoke for a long while.

"I'm sorry, Mr. Lanch," Greene apologized. "We can't solve anything this way."

"I know," replied the stunned, big man.

"We must find a way to help Bobby," Greene offered anew. He

slid his chair back and walked to the window. He bent down and retrieved the folder.

"It's too late," moaned Lanch.

"Please, bring your chair over, and let me show you Bobby's record."

"I know whut's inside," said Lanch. "I ain't been able to he'p Bobby since he come home from the second grade. I couldn't even figure out them little pick-churs he brung home. He cried an' I didn't know whut to do."

With that, the big man buried his face in his rough hands and shook quietly with sobs.

Greene could hear Willie closing the office door, to return silently down the hallway.

He felt very sad for Bobby and for Bobby's father. Yet, at the same time, he knew that Mr. Lanch's appeal for help and genuine sorrow were stalwart strides toward what his own soul cherished. . . . *ἀλήθεια, ἀγαθόν, καλόν.*

SOMETHING HIGHER

Something Higher

The young minister stood quietly beside the curtains at his study window and watched the two men trudging up the road. They would soon be parallel with the parsonage.

He stood in the shadows of the room, where he couldn't be seen. He hoped the men would not stop.

It was cold and overcast outside. A stiff wind stirred the slender branches of the bare maple trees in his yard. The trees' reddish twigs formed a stark contrast against the gray horizon of the winter sky. The scene created an aesthetic wonder in the silence of his soul.

Across the roadway, the steady tug of the wind bowed tall shafts of broom sedge almost to the ground. Beyond the road's ditch, a fallow field dropped off sharply toward a distant line of cedars.

The two men on the road bent their heads into the wind and passed the parsonage without glancing in his direction. He felt relief as he watched them plod out of view.

He sighed and stepped back from the curtains.

In truth, he felt sorry for the men, and for scores like them, who walked up and down the road every day. Twice, he had even seen a young pregnant woman pass by. The first time she was walking. The second time, she was driving an old pickup truck.

So many mills had laid off workers. It happened every Christmas, but this year the layoffs were permanent.

The communities of Donalds, Ware Shoals, Honea Path, and the tiny hamlet of Shoals Junction had been hit the hardest.

In September, the textile plant at Ware Shoals had all but closed. The ailing industry was in a steep recession. The old plant had been forced to dismiss half its work force.

Most of the laid-off workers were drawing unemployment. But the younger men, who had lost their jobs first, had exhausted their benefits. And those who had been unable to find new employment were hard pressed.

As he walked back to his desk, he worried about the recent rash of break-ins and wondered when the parsonage itself would be hit.

Two weeks ago his lawnmower had been stolen. Just this morning, he realized that some of his firewood, which he kept on the carport, had also been pilfered during the night.

He tried to return to his sermon, but his thoughts were preoccupied with the theft of his firewood and the plight of the men on the road. Above all, he was moved, with a special sense of pity, for the woman.

"What can be done?" he wondered aloud. "'You will always have the poor with you,'" he reassured himself. Besides, you have your own work to do and preparations to complete for tonight's service, he reminded himself.

"Good!" he exclaimed aloud. "I'll come back to my message when I can concentrate better."

He rose from his chair, walked around the desk, and out into the living room toward the hall closet.

It was quiet and lonely in the parsonage. For this reason, he often talked out loud to himself. He had to have some anodyne, he reasoned.

He tried not to think about it, but whenever the solitude slipped into his being, as it was doing now, he remembered his young wife and how her sudden death had plunged him into the void.

Nothing had shattered his self-confidence, his quiet sheltered studies, his high and noble idealism, as her death!

He could still see her in his mind. He could sense her presence in the room.

How he wanted to breathe her name! To hold her in his arms!

He fought back the emotion that welled up hot in his throat and lodged in his esophagus.

She had died giving birth to a horribly grotesque infant. It could not be called a child. It was more like a stringy fold of prenatal tissue, an enlarged fetus: twisted, ugly, blue. Something meant to be aborted. Not born.

"We can save it," the doctor said, "but it will never be normal."

He had stared at the doctor in shock.

"You have to know," the doctor said. "I don't like it any more than you."

He had glanced anxiously at his wife. She had been in labor seventeen hours. Her face was pasty, her lips gray. Tears were in her eyes and she was moaning. Suddenly she coughed and gasped for breath.

A nurse hurried the infant away. His wife's body convulsed erratically. Her breathing stopped.

He stood near the end of the delivery table and watched the physician and his staff try desperately to revive her.

She died with them hovering over her.

He could still see himself kneeling beside the grave and having to be led away by Pal Dodson. Six days later, numb and emotionless, he listened again while his superintendent intoned the funeral prayer for a child. . . .

His world had never been the same since. Oh, not that he blamed God! Though he had entered his room and shut the door and had prayed to the Father in secret.

But it was something else. Something more.

It was something he still couldn't accept. Couldn't acknowledge.

Sometimes he would wake up at night in a sweat. Sometimes he would wake up in the darkness and reach for the light. Sometimes he wondered if God existed.

Surely if God existed, he would care. And if he cared, surely he had the power to make things happen otherwise.

That things had not happened otherwise created an uneasiness at the very center of his existence.

He stopped at the closet, glanced back across the silent room, pulled on his coat and hat, and stepped out into the cold.

He strode to the carport, unlocked his Citation, and climbed in. After several turns of the ignition, he started the car.

While he sat there waiting for the engine to warm up, he stared across the lot behind the parsonage. Beyond it, on a raised, graveled right-of-way, loomed, as far as the eye could see, a long, desultory line of idled boxcars.

Between Honea Path and Hodges, the Southern Railroad had

idled hundreds, if not a thousand, old boxcars. They stretched for eighteen miles between the two towns. They formed a ragged, red swaying wall, broken only at intersections and crossroads.

They were a stark witness to the severity of the recession.

It made his own personal tragedy seem small, if not minuscule, when measured against the national crisis, the catastrophic plight of millions of people across the country.

Yet, what is more catastrophic . . . ? he wanted to argue. "Don't make me feel guilty," he whispered. "Don't I have a right to some claim of sorrow I can flee to Thee to share?"

He backed the car down the drive and out onto the road, then drove up to the intersection on highway 178. He bumped over the railcrossing, passed through the awesome gap between the cars, and headed south toward Shoals Junction.

To the west, fenced pastureland still glistened white with frost. Small herds of mixed Angus and Charolais munched hungrily on scattered bunches of hay.

To the east stretched the interminable wall of boxcars.

Two men in denim jackets had backed a pickup truck across the highway's ditch and had parked it beside the cars. They were stripping the cars' interiors of whatever lumber and wood they could find. They were using a crowbar to pry off splintery sections of plywood.

His conscience was piqued with indignation. It was wrong, his mind told him. But these were desperate times. And in desperate times, desperate men do unconscionable things. Still, his mind recoiled at the blatant act.

In less than three minutes, he arrived at his destination. At Shoals Junction, he slowed his Citation, bounced once more over a railcrossing, slipped between a section of uncoupled cars, turned right, and pulled in at Pal's store.

Pal Dodson's store was a low, whitewashed, concrete-block building. It looked like a ramshackle shed that time had abandoned. Dried vines and wind-blown trash hugged its bleak walls.

A large pile of stove wood was heaped near the gas pumps. Peach crates were stacked against the building. Its screen door needed a bottom hinge, and the screen had rusted and split.

Bill got out of the car and walked to the door.

"Well, well, if it isn't the Preacher!" Pal called, as Bill entered the store.

Bill closed the door and nodded respectfully toward the old gentleman.

Pal was wearing a soiled felt hat pushed back high over a shock of his disheveled hair. He hadn't shaved, and his light gray stubble gave a gentle grizzly appearance to his sagging frame. He was chewing on a cigar butt, stuffed tightly between his lips. A teasing mirth twinkled in his eyes.

"Come on over to the fire," Pal grunted. "It's bitter outside."

As Bill followed Pal around the counter to the stove, his eyes surveyed the familiar interior of Pal's establishment.

Blocks of salt for cattle and fifty-pound bags of dog food were stacked near the counter. A table of sorted-through bolts of bright cloth crowded the central aisle. A single light bulb, dangling from a long cord over an old G.E. refrigerator, barely illumined the room.

Only two shelves were stocked with grocery items. The rest were cluttered with old bottles and junk. The room's dirt floor glistened with bottle caps that had dropped to the ground and been trampled under foot into the soil.

"Pal, it's a wonder the health department hasn't condemned you," Bill stated.

"What do you mean?" Pal retorted. "This place is perfect," he grinned, as he spat cigar juice through a crack in the top of the stove.

The "stove" was a rusted, flaking oil drum, set into the dirt floor. A stovepipe, held up with fine wire from the ceiling, served as a flue. It was vented through a boarded-up window, near what had once been the mail-room area in the store.

Bill pulled up a crate near the counter and unbuttoned his coat. He rested his hat on his knee.

"Pal, is everything ready for tonight?" Bill asked.

"Yes, sir," Pal replied. "But we could use some taller candles. The old ones from last year are too short to burn in the windows."

"I could always drive to Greenwood and buy some new ones," Bill offered.

"Well, if you do, I'll see you're reimbursed," Pal said.

Bill was about to respond, when he heard a tug at the door. He turned to behold a young, humbly dressed woman enter the store. He rose politely to his feet and clasped his hat in both hands.

Pal stared momentarily at the girl before he stood up and greeted her. "Come in, Ashley," he said.

The young woman closed the door and glanced apprehensively at Bill.

He recognized her immediately as the girl he had seen walking past the parsonage. She was dressed in a baggy, corduroy-lined denim coat and a maternity dress that was too long for her. She was very pregnant.

As she came to the counter, Bill observed that her left hand was without wedding bands. He looked up from her hand, past a wave of her glossy hair, into her eyes. They were deep brown and gave her face a childlike appearance.

He realized her eyes had been following his gaze. They both blushed at the same time.

"I'm . . . Bill Whiteford," he said.

"Yes," she replied. "I pass your parsonage on the way to town. I'm Ashley Simms."

There was only a trace of upcountry accent to her speech. A gracefulness softened her red-flushed cheeks. He had not caressed or loved a woman since his wife's death.

She turned and addressed Pal. "Mr. Dodson, Aunt Tibbie's phone's out again, and I need to call the Greenwood clinic before they close."

"Yes, ma'am. Help yourself!" Pal said.

She opened her purse and took out two quarters.

"Heavens no!" Pal grunted, taking the cigar butt out of his mouth to keep from having to pick up her money. "Dial anywhere you want. My phone's on the Greenwood exchange."

"Thank you," she replied, as she reached for the telephone.

Bill didn't want to appear rude by overhearing her conversation, so he put on his hat and walked toward the door.

"I need to check on something in the car," he said. "I'll be back."

Outside in the cold, Bill shivered, rebuttoned his coat, and pumped his arms to keep warm. The gray sky overhead was furrowed with low, soft, dark clouds. He estimated it would sleet by dusk. If it did, it would be the first white Christmas he had seen in years.

He walked around Pal's gas pumps to stare at the Simms girl's truck. It was an old, black high-cab Ford pickup. Its running boards were rusting out and its windshield wipers needed blades. The door on the driver's side was bent in. He wondered how it had ever passed inspection.

Suddenly he heard the girl's laughter and Pal's voice. They had caught him gawking at the truck.

He was about to defend himself, when the girl winced, bent slightly to one side, and gently cradled her bulge with her left hand. With her right hand, she held to the truck's bed. Her flushed face reddened deeper.

"You'd better let me put some gasoline in this truck," Pal grunted. "You'll be needing it soon."

"I guess you're right," she replied.

"Climb up in the cab," Pal ordered her with a gruff tenderness. "You can pay me later."

Bill hurried to the driver's door to assist her. He opened the door and held her left arm. She climbed up into the cab and wedged herself behind the big steering wheel.

"Thank you," she said in a low whisper.

He pressed her arm gently before he released it. He closed the door, as best it would shut. Then he stepped back and walked around the bed of the truck to rejoin Pal.

After the girl had driven away, Bill reentered the store with Pal.

"Tell me about her," Bill said. "She's a very pretty girl."

"What do you mean? I should say so!" Pal grunted. The old man drew a long breath and put a fresh cigar in his mouth.

"Don't you ever light those things?" Bill mused.

"Naw, just eat 'em! Live longer that way," Pal retorted. The old storekeeper smiled, sat down, and eyed Bill thoughtfully.

"I've no right to tell you what to do, but she is pretty," Pal began. "She was engaged to a boy at the mill. But when the plant first laid off people, he disappeared. Was no 'count anyway, though. But he sure messed up her life."

Bill listened with painful interest.

"Comes from a fine family," Pal explained. "Her father worked for the Southern. He was killed in a derailment. Her mother died about six years ago. Her Aunt Tibbie took her in and helped her finish college.

"She even taught school for a year. Then she met that bum!"

"Yeah," Bill concurred. "Well, I guess I'll go on to Greenwood," he sighed. He stood up and patted Pal on the shoulder. "Take care," he thanked the old gentleman.

The drive to Greenwood passed quickly. All Bill could think of was Ashley.

Somewhere in college he had read Sartre's statement that "evil is irredeemable." Once evil is done, its consequences can't be reversed. The dead can't be raised, anguish forgotten, scars eradicated.

That had left a deep impression on him. And he had no quarrel with it.

Yet, if the New Testament were true, evil *shall not* have the last word. It doesn't even have to have the last word now.

He wanted so much for that to be true of Ashley. Wasn't that, after all, the meaning of the Incarnation, which he and his congregation were about to celebrate?

He guessed he was still an idealist, but a more sober one, he hoped.

"Evil shall not have the last word," he whispered aloud.

He passed the A.R.P. Church, which LeRoy Jenkins had purchased. The evangelist Jenkins was in prison. It made him reflect on the ministry.

The church can be so irrelevant, he had to admit. Other than creating guilt, salving a few consciences, and reinforcing prejudices, what genuine transformation do we generate? he asked himself.

He wanted to answer, "None!" But that would be giving evil the last word.

He parked his car on the Square near June Elmblad's store and bought the largest remaining red candles she had.

On his way out of town, he ate lunch at Hardee's. A Mennonite couple seated nearby bowed their heads for grace. It made him feel guilty that he hadn't.

South of Shoals Junction, he stopped at the church and arranged the cranberry-colored candles in the windows.

When he arrived at the parsonage, it seemed emptier than ever. He could not get the Simms girl off his mind.

"Why can't I have her?" he whispered. "What would be evil about that? Nothing!" he replied. "But how? How can it be done?" he muttered, as he settled in behind his desk.

Finally, after a great loss of time, he managed to put the pregnant girl out of his thoughts and return to his meditation. He would call it "God's Last Word."

But once he wrote the title down, he felt uneasy. He scratched it out and retitled it, "Something Higher." After all, who can speak God's last word but God?

He barely completed his meditation by dusk. He had to be at the church by 6:15.

He bundled up, returned to the study for his robe, worshipbook, and notes, and, on his way back through the living room, turned on several lamps. Hopefully, that would dissuade burglars. But he doubted it. They always seemed to have the "last word."

When he stepped out into the night, a fine swirl of snow stung him in the face. The flakes were tiny, light, and dry, and sifted down rapidly. They seemed to descend from everywhere. They enveloped the dark night in their splendorous way.

He stopped and held up his hand to catch them. Beads of sleet glistened on his glove. That they would create a driving hazard seemed less of an evil than the wonder they evoked.

He crunched across the icy darkness to the carport. He threw his robe, notes, and book into the back seat, and started the car. As he backed out onto the road, he realized an inch or more of sleet had already fallen.

He could see car lights in his rearview mirror. They were but specks. The car appeared to be slipping on the road.

He knew he should wait to see if it might go off in the ditch. But he was late, as it was. He shifted his car into second and eased slowly up the road toward the highway.

The lights behind him angled crazily out of sight.

He had completed his sermon and was administering the elements, when it occurred to him that the distant lights he had seen in his rearview mirror might have been those of Ashley's truck.

What if her time had come? What if she were trying to make it to Greenwood?

Fool! You are crazy! he thought to himself.

The people who knelt to receive the cup looked up at him with puzzlement in their eyes.

When the service was over, he suddenly seized Pal by the shoulders. "I must get home!" he announced.

He hurried to his car. He brushed the icy snow off his windshield with his bare left hand. He jumped in and waved a hasty farewell to a group of worshipers who were trying to thank him for his message.

"It was well done," they complimented him.

"Thank you," he mumbled as he drove away.

"Well, what a fine send-off that is!" he heard them complain.

His temples throbbed with embarrassment.

It had stopped sleeting. But the snow was still falling. The flakes were large and wet. He wiped the cold moisture off the inside of his windshield. Ashley's truck didn't even have blades.

"Don't panic!" he rebuked himself. "She's probably safe and warm at home."

Still, he had lost one wife. He didn't want to lose "another," he whispered.

On his left, he passed group after little group of cattle, huddled up against the fence line. Snow and sleet sparkled on their coats. Their breath created an iridescent steam about them.

On his right loomed the dark specter of silent, empty boxcars.

He thought he would never reach his own road. He bumped softly across the snow-filled railcrossing. The tires slipped on the icy rails as the Citation passed between the somber cars.

When he arrived at the parsonage, he was relieved to see no black truck, or any vehicle, on the road or in the ditch. At least, if one were there, it was beyond his sight in the storm.

He pulled the car into the carport, over the light crusty snow that the wind had blown into it. As he did, the headlights illumined the faint outline of footsteps.

"Not again!" he thought. "Prowlers."

He left his car engine running and stepped out to examine the footprints. They were small. Hardly a man's. Powdery snow had sifted into the icy prints. He judged them to be about an hour old.

He walked around the carport to discover that the prints led from his walkway, across the edge of the apron, and out through the lot, behind the parsonage. They disappeared in the direction of the boxcars.

He was seized with anguish. He hurried to the car, reached under the front seat, and groped for his flashlight.

He found it and turned it on, but nothing happened. He thumped it hard against the palm of his gloved hand. Still, no light.

The batteries were dead. He shook it violently and flung it out into the snow.

He left his engine running, headlights on, and hurried across the lot toward the boxcars. He was panting when he reached them. He looked for more footprints, but couldn't find any.

He stooped down. He peered under the nearest boxcar. "Ashley!" he called. "Are you here?"

There was no sound, save for the wind.

He tried the door, but it was locked.

He ran to a second car, but its entrance was too high, even for him.

He turned and stared back toward the parsonage and the headlights. He realized the snow had stopped falling. It had mantled the ground with a rough glaze. The dim impression of prints led this way, then disappeared.

He looked up. The clouds were drifting away. And the sky was beginning to fill with silent, scintillating stars.

He ran to a third car. "Ashley! Ashley!" he repeated.

He listened, but there was no answer.

He bolted to the fourth car. Its entrance was low, and its great door was open.

"Ashley! Are you here?"

He thought he heard a movement. He pulled himself up into the darkness of the car. His own breathing and heartbeat drowned out momentarily all other sounds.

"Ashley!" he whispered. "It's me. Bill."

He heard a faint moan. "Please, help me," a young woman's voice groaned.

He crawled in the direction of her voice. Outside, the starlight silhouetted the outline of the boxcar's stark doorway. It was like peering through a great, black hole, into the Infinite.

"Ashley," he whispered, as he found her and eased his arm under her head. "It's all right," he kissed her.

She took his hand and squeezed it with all her might. Her eyes glistened with tears. "The baby's coming. I can't help it," she said.

"Let it come," he urged her.

"Oh," she groaned. "Ohh!" she screamed.

He yanked off his coat and knelt between her legs. He ripped out the coat's lining and wedged the coat under her body.

She had fully dilated. The starlight dimly illumined the drama.

She coughed and screamed with all her might.

"Push!" he shouted, as she gave birth to a glossy, wet infant. It whimpered and thrashed its arms as he wrapped it in the warm lining. He held it up to his chest in the light.

"It's beautiful!" he uttered. "It's perfectly formed!"

Then he laid it gently in her arms and untied a shoelace, in order to tie off the umbilical cord.

It is early summer. Iris blooms along the edge of the carport. The maple trees are in full leaf.

In the parsonage, the sound of a mother's lullaby emanates from the nursery. Bill lifts up his face from his studies and listens.

Suddenly, he is jolted with surprise. It is the sound of freight cars, bumping violently together on the railroad. He turns from his desk to stare out his rear study window.

Switchmen from the Southern Railroad are recoupling the cars. A diesel engine is pulling them away.

"No!" he whispers, as he watches the boxcars sway and lumber slowly along the tracks.

"No, no!" he sighs, as he rises slowly to his feet. "You were my witnesses," he addresses them. "You can't go now."

The rails groan and the cars move faster.

"Who will believe me?" he asks aloud. "You were my testimony that evil does not have. . . ."

The cars rumble out of sight.

All is silent again. Save for the sound of his breathing. And the rustle of Ashley behind him.

THE GIRL IN THE POLKA DOT DRESS

The Girl in the Polka Dot Dress

The woman who lay in the bed had lost consciousness again, or at least had drifted into sleep. Her husband was not certain which. But he could tell she was still breathing from the slight rise and fall of the limp gown on her chest. He held her left hand in his and caressed it worriedly.

He knew she would regain consciousness, but if not tonight, or tomorrow, or tomorrow night, she would finally lose consciousness, period. And he would lose her forever.

He bent forward and kissed her hand and held it as tenderly as he could. Then he wiped some of the light perspiration from her face and brushed her thin hair back gently with his hand.

She was thirty-eight. He was forty-two. She was dying of cancer. He could not keep her much longer. Then he would have to let her go. He would have to give her back. But he would not let her go or give her back until he had to.

He stared lovingly at her face. The last weeks had been the hardest. She had lost twelve pounds just in the past month, and her neck was wrinkled and gray.

Her cheekbones stood up and her mouth fell away like an old woman's chin. But in his heart he saw her as he had always seen her: as the girl in the blue polka dot dress, smiling, looking up at him, as she stood near the mantelpiece that evening at the party.

He took a deep breath, released her hand, and sat back in the chair beside the bed.

He had walked her home after the party. It had been a warm September night, and he had held her hand all the way. He had teased her for the way she said "house" and "about." But that had been eighteen years ago.

All through that fall he had dated her as if each night were the last and there would be no tomorrow.

He smiled to himself, proud of the persistency with which he had courted her. He could remember the night he gave her the delicate gold bracelet while they sat in the VW beside the quiet lake at Richmond's Byrd Park.

He could remember the afternoon they visited Williamsburg and how they had run laughing together from the Governor's Palace because of the histrionics of their silly guide and the comical way in which she had reenacted Patrick Henry's speech.

He could still feel her in his arms at the Crater and would always remember that tour of the battlefields of Richmond and the quiet woods near Malvern Hill.

By November he could never leave her. And on the twentieth of that month they were wed in a simple ceremony in the chapel of a church just off Monument Boulevard, overlooking the statues of Robert E. Lee and J.E.B. Stuart.

That winter they lived in a small apartment on Second Avenue. It was upstairs in a widow's house. She had rented them three rooms: a kitchen, a living room, and a tiny bedroom, with a bath just off the hall stairs.

"Your heat is what you make it!" she had called to them as they looked down at her from the balcony.

He had pressed his wife's hand and both had laughed. And all through that winter they laughed and loved and laughed each time they made love, for the apartment literally had no heat save what they "made."

The bathroom had a tiny electric heater of which only two coils worked. The bedroom had none. The gas fireplace in the living room was unvented and thus could not be used. And the pilot light on the gas range in the kitchen kept going out.

Without radio or TV, they spent that first winter's evenings in bed, each propped up on a pillow, she working crossword puzzles while he outlined books and wrote reports for his master's degree.

By spring she was pregnant. She would slip out of bed before he woke up to relief herself of the nausea. He would hear her flushing the commode.

By late August she was not doing well. The doctor ordered her to bed. He was still in graduate school, and her secretarial job with the governor's office was their only income.

The heat in the upstairs apartment was unbearable. She fainted climbing the stairs. He tried cooling her with damp cloths that he carried from the bathroom.

Without air conditioning, she lay on the bed and sweltered in misery. He wanted to buy a fan, but they didn't have enough money. As a last resort, the doctor prescribed a bottle of paregoric.

The following night she began hemorrhaging, and he carried her in his arms down the stairs and out to the Volkswagen.

It was 3:00 a.m. The street was quiet, the lamplight dim, the night black and hot.

He drove to a pay telephone booth and called the doctor. The doctor cursed him and told him to bring her to the hospital just down the street from the Stuart statue.

He remembered how pale she was when he came back to see her and how she held his hand and cried. She was so young and beautiful. That night when he climbed the steps to the apartment he lay on the floor in the living room and wept.

He wondered if they would always be poor. Would he find a job when he completed his degree? Should he drop out and try to find work and get her out of that apartment? What should he do?

By fall he was teaching school. They were living in another part of the city, in an apartment with four rooms. This time it had heat, but the utility bills left scarcely enough for groceries and insurance.

That Christmas they could not afford a tree. They drove to several different lots but gave up when they couldn't find anything under three dollars.

She baked some raisin-filled cookies. They bought a quart of eggnog and made it last as long as they could by diluting it with powdered skim milk.

He took two coat hangers and bent them together in the form of a pyramid. She decorated the frame with a necklace of bright plastic beads. Then they bought a nineteen-cent package of tinsel and covered the "tree" with the shiny foil.

The following spring she was pregnant again. That summer they bought a fan. That fall she gave birth to a little boy, who died on her stomach in the delivery room.

Sometimes when they were lying in bed together she would remember that moment and talk about it.

"The doctor just plopped him up on my stomach. He was so tiny, blue, and cold."

"Why?" he would ask her. "Why did he ever do it?"

"Maybe he did it because my stomach was the warmest surface in the room . . ."

That winter the governor's office reduced its staff, and she lost her job. So they had to give up their apartment for something less desirable.

They moved to the edge of town and rented a trailer. She found work as a waitress in a truck stop. He applied for an assistant principal's position but was turned down on the grounds that he had not completed his master's degree and therefore lacked aggressive drive.

That spring he began working at night in one of Richmond's malls. And throughout the summer he kept it as a part-time job.

Between his teaching, her waitress work, and his part-time job, they were seldom together anymore. Sometimes on Sunday when she was off, they would drive to the Boulevard and park the VW by the church and take long strolls past the statues and the huge old homes that looked out across the grassy median.

Whenever they could, they ate at Morton's Tea Room for a dollar and a quarter. They were always having to count pennies. They still owed the doctor from the time of the miscarriage and had buried their child in an unmarked grave in the Hollywood Cemetery.

"One of these days, darling, life will get better," he would say. "Somehow, somewhere, we'll break this chain of poverty."

"I know," she would smile. "We're young and we'll survive it. And we'll buy us a home on the Boulevard!"

And so they would walk arm in arm, up the sidewalk, along the Boulevard, and listen to the traffic clap over the old pavement stones.

Sometimes they would walk down the median and in the autumn kick up the leaves and throw them at each other.

"We will not let bad luck or poverty get us down!" they would laugh and assure one another.

That winter he finally secured a position in a better school and a raise to accompany it. They left the trailer and rented a small house on the west side of town.

They lived close to the James River and would drive out on Sundays to watch it flow by and ebb around the great outcroppings that ribbed the middle of the channel.

In the summer they visited the beach. They retraced their visit to Williamsburg. They bought a set of blue onion china at the old warehouse in Toano and ate fudge at the candy shop near the campus of William and Mary.

One day that fall when he returned home he found her crying. She had been to the doctor earlier to see about having another baby.

"What did he say?" he asked her.

"He said, 'No.' We must never try again. There is something wrong with my cervix. And my uterus is in the wrong position. It needs to be tied back."

"Surely our insurance will cover that!" he said. But when he asked his principal to examine the policy, he learned it would not.

That evening when he told her the news she sat by the window in the kitchen and stared silently out at the gathering haze and dusk.

It was very beautiful that winter. December was cold and snowy. They bought a small fir tree and decorated it with lights and silver ornaments. She bought him a turtleneck sweater and slippers, and he bought her a bathrobe from England made of one-hundred-percent wool.

She baked a spice cake and turkey, and he splurged by bringing home a bottle of champagne. They sat in the living room that Christmas evening and listened to records he had bought on sale while working at the mall the previous year.

On Christmas day they rode out to the river. It was freezing cold. Thick slabs of ice had formed along the bank and part-way out across the river. Giant icicles hung from branches and debris lodged on the outcroppings. The cold water danced in the sunlight as it churned by.

They made a snowman and threw snowballs at each other. That night they drove downtown to a Toddle House and had eggs and apple pie and coffee for supper.

The years came and passed. A touch of gray appeared in her hair. She was as lovely as ever, if not more so than when he had married her, only at times she seemed pale and was often quite weak.

At first he did not notice it. Then one morning, while he was slipping out of bed and trying not to wake her, he noted that her face seemed sallow and her cheeks sunken.

He meant to say something about it and forgot.

Several months passed. Then he realized she was losing weight. It was most apparent in her face and arms and breasts.

"Are you all right, darling?" he asked.

"I think so," she said. "Though sometimes I feel swollen deep inside and sore, and then it seems to go away."

"I think you should see a doctor. How long has it been since your last checkup?"

"I can't remember," she said. "We're always so tight for money I hate to go as long as I feel all right."

"We should have had your uterus tied back," he said. "We should have borrowed the money, whatever it might have cost. Somehow we would have paid it back."

"Maybe it's just as well that we didn't," she said. "It's been all we can do to survive."

"I know," he said. "But you need to go and see about yourself."

She promised him she would.

"Please!" he begged her.

"I will," she replied.

It was now the spring of their eighteenth year of marriage. They had driven up into the mountains for the weekend. They had stopped briefly at Monticello and then had driven on to Staunton for the night.

Early the next morning they drove on up to Monterey for the maple syrup festival. Ice still glazed sections of the highway and deep patches of snow lay in the coves.

The road was steep and curvy, and when his wife began to grow sick he thought it was from the car's motion and the winding interminable curves.

When they arrived in Monterey they stopped for breakfast at a high school where a group of townspeople were serving pancakes, sausage, and fresh maple syrup. He was famished but could not eat when he realized how sick and weak she had become.

They rested for awhile. Then they drove out to one of the farms to watch them tap the huge maple trees for their delectable sap.

They were standing in the cold air by a long steaming tank, enjoying the heat of the fire, when suddenly she caught hold of his shoulder, swayed, and fainted in his arms. . . .

He heard her stir in the bed. The sound of her breathing broke his reverie. He was glad she was gaining consciousness again.

He bent forward and took her hand. She opened her eyes and smiled. He kissed her tenderly on the cheek and brushed back her hair. A droplet of sweat dripped off his fingers onto the pillow.

"Can I get you anything?" he asked.

She shook her head no and quietly studied his eyes and face and reached up with her right hand and held it against his cheek. He kissed her fingers and laid her hand in his near her breasts. She smiled and closed her eyes again.

He glanced at his watch. It was 2:30 a.m. His own eyes begged for sleep, but he could not and would not leave her. He felt tired, but he told himself he must remain strong for her.

He thought of the months that had passed since their visit to Monterey. That he had gotten her back at all seemed a miracle. That she had survived as long as she had seemed another. And after the hysterectomy and the cobalt and all of the chemotherapy . . . that she was still alive and had kept most of her hair! Was it just possible . . . ?

"O God," he whispered to himself, "could it be a sign? Can it be a sign that this cup will pass from us and I can have her back? Please, God. Let this cup pass from us!"

But when he looked up at her lips and cheeks, he knew this precious cup would pass from him and would be no more.

He listened to her sleep. Soft, sweet, and lovely sleep. O balm from pain! O mortal anodyne!

He could remember that first morning he awoke and felt her beside him in the bed and had listened to her breathing. It seemed so long ago. But he remembered it as if it had only been that morning.

He knew now that every morning he should henceforth wake he would remember that morning and would instinctively reach out for her in his heart.

He lay his head on the bed and thought of those first years of poverty from which they had never recovered. Why? Why does fate deal so harshly with love? But his heart fought back, No, no! How beautiful is love!

Still if he had never married her, wouldn't her life be better? What had he given her? What had he brought her?

"Eighteen years of marginal poverty," he whispered aloud. "And two tiny lives. Two lost infant lives that moved in thy womb and that both our hands and hearts felt with wonder and awe!"

And eighteen years of dreams and struggles, he reminded himself, only briefly broken by the reprieve of joy.

Why hadn't she left him? Why had she stayed? Why had she taken it?

In all that time she had never complained. She was always there. Always faithful.

Why hadn't they quarreled? Why couldn't something have happened to have made her life fuller and happier? Why?

He lifted his head off the bed and looked at her longingly. He glanced at his watch again. 3:00 a.m. He leaned back in the chair and closed his eyes.

When he awoke, the sun was shining into the room. A narrow band of light had slipped past the curtains and the shade and was filling the world with a new day.

Suddenly he became aware of the stillness! It had slipped into his soul and pervaded the whole room.

He looked anxiously toward his wife. She was lying on her side, utterly motionless. Her mouth was slightly agape. Her eyes were partially closed. Her hands were outstretched on the bedspread toward him.

She was dead.

He fell to his knees and clasped her hands.

"Darling, darling!" he cried. "My love, my love!" he whispered.

An indescribable anguish of loss came upon him. He wept uncontrollably. He buried his face in the bedspread and soaked it with his tears. Deep down in his heart something gave way that could not be consoled.

After a long time, he began to search within himself for something to which he might cling. In the silence and agony of that moment he could see her again as he had always seen her and always would—as the girl in the polka dot dress.

Then from the depths of his being a sense of love and of having been loved overwhelmed him and he remembered these words:

Love bears all things, believes all things, hopes all things, endures all things.

Love never ends.